WHISPERS OF THE
TEA LEAVES
ROMANCE AND REBELLION

JITU MISHRA

Vidya Publishing Inc

Whispers of the Tea Leaves

Jitu Mishra

VIDYA
PUBLISHING INC.

Vidya Publishing Inc.

Wishpers of the Tea Leaves
Author: Jitu Mishra

ISBN: 9781998475599

First Edition:	April, 2025
Published by:	**Dr. Tanmay Panda &**
	Dr. Sunanda Mishra Panda
	Vidya Publishing Inc.,
	Toronto, Canada || Bhubaneswar, India
Website:	**www.vidyapublishing.com**
Email:	vidyapublishinginc@gmail.com
Cell:	+1 6478389884
India Contact:	Nirmalya Garden, Plot 516/1719, House 10,
	KIIT Post Office, Bhubaneswar - 751024
Cell:	+91 8984131810
Cover Design:	**Jitu Mishra**
	Printed in India, Biswanath Enterprises

Price: ` 499 /-

Author's Note

Writing Whispers of the Tea Leaves has been a journey across time, culture, and history—a story born from the shadows of colonialism, the resilience of indigenous people, and the quiet power of love.

At its heart, this novel is about freedom—not just political freedom, but the freedom to choose one's destiny, to love beyond borders, and to reclaim what was taken.

The History Behind the Fiction

While this is a work of historical fiction, the exploitation of Assam's tea plantations was real. The British East India Company's control over the region was marked by forced labor, land seizures, and a monopoly that shaped the global tea trade. The workers, many of whom were migrants from Central India, faced inhumane conditions, and yet their contributions built one of the most lucrative industries of the empire.

But resistance was also real.

There were quiet acts of defiance, escapes, and small rebellions—stories that history has largely forgotten. This novel is, in part, a tribute to those unseen voices.

Emily and Rajveer: A Love Beyond Empire

Emily's journey is a reflection of many who questioned their privilege and chose to stand with the oppressed rather than against them. Her transformation from a privileged British woman to a revolutionary in Assam mirrors the way history has often been shaped—by those who dared to cross lines that were never meant to exist.

Rajveer embodies the spirit of Assam—rooted in its land, its traditions, and its quiet but fierce resistance. His love for tea is not just about cultivation but about identity. The British may have controlled Assam's plantations, but they never owned its soil.

A Story for Today

While the days of British colonial rule are gone, the exploitation of land, labor, and resources continues in new forms. The tea industry, though modernized, still grapples with ethical concerns about fair wages, working conditions, and sustainability.

The story of Assam is not just a historical tale—it is a reminder that history lingers in the very things we consume. Every cup of tea holds within it a journey—from the hands that plucked its leaves to the stories of the people behind it.

Acknowledgments

This book would not have been possible without countless historical accounts, oral traditions, and the inspiration drawn from Assam's landscape, culture, and people.

To those who have preserved the history of the tea trade —scholars, storytellers, and the workers themselves—this novel is my humble tribute.

To the readers who have followed Emily and Rajveer's journey, thank you. May you always taste the whispers of history in the simplest things.

With gratitude,
Jitu Mishra

Dedication

To the unseen hands that have plucked the leaves, to the voices history tried to silence, and to the land that has endured.

This story is for you.

And to those who still listen for the whispers of the past, may you always find them in the rustling of the leaves, the rhythm of the earth, and the quiet strength of love.

Jitu Mishra

Chapter One:
Arrival in the Land of Mist and Green

Whispers of the Tea Leaves

The steamship cut through the thick mist that hung over the mighty Brahmaputra, its whistle piercing the silence of the early morning. Emily Davenport stood at the deck's edge, her hands gripping the iron railing, watching the dense jungle stretch endlessly beyond the riverbanks. Assam. This was to be her new home, far from the drawing rooms of London and the manicured gardens of Calcutta.

The air was thick with moisture, carrying the unfamiliar scent of damp earth, spice, and something bitter—something sharp. It tickled her senses in a way that felt both strange and intoxicating. It was the scent of tea.

She glanced at her husband, Henry Davenport, who stood beside her, reviewing plantation documents with an air of practiced indifference. He was a man of rigid posture and even firmer convictions, a respected tea planter under the British East India Company. He had spoken of Assam as a wild and untamed place, a land that had to be subdued like a disobedient child.

Emily had seen it differently.

From the moment their ship had entered the Assam Valley, the landscape had bewitched her. The rolling tea plantations, the thick forests hiding secrets older than any British rule, the Brahmaputra carving its way through the land like a forgotten legend—it was nothing like the cold, grey streets of England. Here, life pulsed beneath the surface, ancient and unshaken by the empire her husband served so faithfully.

They disembarked at a small wooden jetty where a waiting palanquin stood, draped in white muslin to keep out the sun. The workers, dark-skinned and wiry, kept their heads bowed as Henry barked instructions. Emily's gaze, however, fell upon one man who did not look away.

He was standing apart from the rest, dressed in a loose white dhoti and a faded red gamcha draped over one shoulder. His eyes, dark and steady, met hers with quiet defiance. He was not like the others, who shuffled about in forced servitude. There was something about him—an air of belonging, of knowing the land in a way that no Englishman ever could.

"Get in, Emily," Henry commanded, barely sparing her a glance.

She hesitated, then stepped into the palanquin, the muslin curtain falling around her. Yet, even as the bearers lifted her onto their shoulders, she felt his gaze linger, just as hers did.

The journey to the plantation took nearly half a day. The road was barely more than a muddy trail, winding through dense forests where the sounds of unseen creatures echoed. Occasionally, they passed villages—clusters of bamboo huts raised on stilts, smoke rising from earthen hearths, children peering curiously at the passing procession.

Jitu Mishra

By the time they reached the estate, the sun was a burning orange disk, casting long shadows across the tea gardens.

Davenport Tea Estate

It was vast, larger than Emily had imagined, its green slopes undulating like the waves of the sea. Workers moved in synchronized motion, plucking the delicate tea leaves and dropping them into woven baskets. Overseers patrolled the fields on horseback, their whips resting against their saddles like silent threats.

Henry gestured proudly. "This is what we've built, Emily. The lifeblood of the empire."

She did not answer.

Something in the way the workers moved—their bent backs, their weary steps—did not align with the grandeur Henry saw.

And then, she saw him again.

The man from the jetty.

He was standing at the far end of the field, speaking to a group of laborers. His voice was low, but the others listened intently, their eyes flickering with something that looked almost like hope.

Jitu Mishra

Their eyes met once more.

This time, Emily did not look away.

Somewhere in the whispers of the tea leaves, a story had already begun.

Chapter Two:
The First Cup

Whispers of the Tea Leaves

Emily sat in the grand dining hall of the Davenport Estate, her hands resting lightly on the porcelain tea cup before her. The candlelit chandelier flickered against the dark wooden beams overhead, casting shadows across the grand room. The long table, set with polished silverware and bone china, felt excessive in the silence that stretched between her and Henry.

Her husband sat across from her, engrossed in a ledger of plantation accounts. He barely acknowledged her presence as he scribbled notes in the margins, muttering numbers under his breath.

"You must start learning how things work here," he finally spoke, his tone firm, his eyes not leaving the paper. "The estate, the workers, the tea processing— these are the foundations of our success."

Emily hesitated, stirring her tea absentmindedly. "I want to see the plantation," she said softly.

Henry glanced up at her, his brows slightly furrowed. "The fields?"

She nodded. "Yes. I should understand how tea is grown if I'm to be a part of this life."

A shadow of irritation flickered across his face. "The fields are no place for a lady, Emily. It is hot, dirty, and filled with laborers who wouldn't know how to address you properly."

Whispers of the Tea Leaves

"I don't mind," she said, meeting his gaze.

Henry sighed and leaned back in his chair. "Fine," he said, closing the ledger. "You may see the processing rooms first. The actual labor is not something you need to concern yourself with."

Emily said nothing, merely sipping her tea. But in her mind, she had already decided.

She would see the fields.

The Tea Fields at Dawn

The next morning, the estate awoke before the sun. The mist curled through the valleys, hovering low over the rows of green tea bushes. The smell of damp earth and fresh leaves filled the air as workers, dressed in simple cotton garments, moved in synchronized motions—pluck, twist, drop—their baskets growing heavier with each handful of leaves.

Emily stepped carefully onto the narrow dirt path that wound through the plantation, her lace-trimmed parasol offering little protection against the thick morning air. A few workers lifted their heads at the sight of her—a rare spectacle in their world of toil.

Then, she saw him again.

The tea worker from the riverbank.

Whispers of the Tea Leaves

He was standing a short distance away, speaking to an elderly woman who was plucking leaves at an even, practiced pace. His posture was relaxed, but there was an unspoken authority about him, a quiet power in the way the others listened when he spoke.

Emily hesitated. The workers avoided eye contact with her, but he did not.

Their gazes met, and in that moment, something shifted —a silent recognition of an unseen thread that tied them together.

She took a step forward.

"Memsaab, this way," a voice interrupted.

It was Mr. Hastings, Henry's overseer, a broad-shouldered man with a ruddy face. He gestured for her to follow him toward the drying sheds.

Emily forced herself to look away from the tea worker and nodded. But as she walked past, she caught a whisper on the breeze—low, melodic, spoken in a tongue she did not yet understand.

She didn't need to.

It was not a greeting, nor a farewell.

It was simply a presence, a whisper carried by the tea leaves.

Whispers of the Tea Leaves

A Taste of Something Different

Later that evening, as the estate settled into its quiet rhythm, Emily found herself alone in the kitchen. The servants had long finished their tasks, leaving behind rows of neatly stacked tea tins.

She reached for one, opening the lid to release a soft, earthy aroma, nothing like the sharp, perfumed teas she had grown accustomed to.

Carefully, she took a few leaves and brewed a cup over the fire, just as she had seen the tea worker do—without milk, without sugar, just pure infusion.

The first sip was unexpected.

It was bold, unrefined, untouched by British hands. It tasted like Assam itself—wild, rich, untamed.

And in that moment, she knew.

The story of this land was not written in the ledgers Henry kept. It was not found in the grand estates or the colonial tea rooms of London.

It was here, in the hands of those who plucked the leaves, in the whispers carried on the evening breeze.

And it had only just begun.

Chapter Three:
Between Two Worlds

The scent of freshly plucked tea leaves lingered in the air as Emily stepped out onto the verandah of the Davenport Estate. The morning sun, though still low, cast a golden glow over the rolling tea fields, where workers moved in synchronized rhythm, their fingers nimble as they plucked the delicate leaves. The rhythmic sound of their woven baskets filling was almost hypnotic.

From the distance, she saw him again.

The tea worker, the one whose gaze had met hers in the fields, stood among the laborers, his posture calm yet commanding. He was not like the others—he moved with quiet authority, his presence unshaken by the colonial world that surrounded him.

Emily felt a strange pull—a curiosity that went beyond mere observation. There was something about him, something that the British world around her either did not see or refused to acknowledge.

Her husband's voice broke through her thoughts.

The Tea Tasting

"Emily, you must learn the proper way of evaluating tea," Henry said, his tone clipped and efficient. "We will be visiting the tasting room."

She turned to face him, her mind still half in the fields. "Tasting room?"

Whispers of the Tea Leaves

"Yes. The quality of our tea determines its value in the market. You must understand how to assess its strength, aroma, and texture."

Minutes later, Emily found herself inside a cool, dimly lit room, a long wooden table stretching before her. Rows of china cups filled with brewed tea sat neatly arranged, their colors varying from pale amber to deep brown. A British overseer, Hastings, stood at the head of the table, carefully swirling a spoon in one of the cups.

"The trick," he explained, "is to take a sharp, quick sip, rolling it over the tongue to evaluate its depth." He demonstrated, making a loud slurping sound before spitting the tea into a brass spittoon.

Emily hesitated before following suit, the bitter liquid spreading across her tongue. It was different from the tea she had brewed in the kitchen the night before—this was sharper, more processed, stripped of its raw essence.

She frowned slightly.

"The best leaves," Henry continued, ignoring her reaction, "are those that produce a brisk, malty flavor—strong enough to withstand milk and sugar, as the British prefer."

Emily nodded absently, but her thoughts were elsewhere.

She wanted to taste the tea from the fields, not the one prepared for British markets.

Whispers of the Tea Leaves

A Chance Meeting

That evening, as the estate settled into its familiar rhythm, Emily found herself walking along the edge of the plantation, where the structured rows of tea bushes met the wild jungle beyond.

And then, he was there.

The tea worker stood at the foot of an old banyan tree, his hands resting at his sides as if he had been waiting.

She hesitated. Should she turn back? Speak? Leave things as they were?

Before she could decide, he inclined his head slightly.

"You do not drink tea like them."

His voice was steady, rich—spoken in English, but with an accent that carried the rhythms of Assam.

Emily's breath caught. She had not expected him to speak to her.

"I—" she faltered, then steadied herself. "No, I don't."

He studied her for a moment, then reached into a small cloth pouch tied at his waist. He pulled out a few dried tea leaves—deep green, unprocessed.

"This is real tea," he said, holding them out to her. "Not the kind they send to England."

Emily took the leaves hesitantly, her fingers brushing against his palm for the briefest moment.

A strange sense of understanding passed between them, something that had no words but was deeply felt.

She wanted to ask his name, but before she could, he stepped back into the shadows of the trees.

Emily stood there for a long time, the tea leaves cradled in her palm, the distant hum of the plantation behind her.

And for the first time since she had arrived in Assam, she felt truly awake.

Chapter Four:
Secrets in the Leaves

Whispers of the Tea Leaves

The tea leaves sat wrapped in a small silk handkerchief on Emily's writing desk. She had placed them there the previous night after returning from her encounter with the tea worker beneath the banyan tree, but sleep had evaded her. The touch of his fingers as he had handed them to her—the quiet defiance in his gaze—lingered in her mind.

She ran her fingertips over the delicate leaves, inhaling their deep, earthy scent. They were unlike the processed, carefully sorted tea she had seen in the plantation's tasting room. These were untouched, raw—tea in its purest form.

Emily closed her eyes, remembering his words.

"This is real tea. Not the kind they send to England."

A Morning of Expectations

The usual morning routine at the Davenport Estate unfolded as expected. Emily sat across from Henry at breakfast, the clinking of silverware against porcelain the only sound between them.

Henry, as always, was engrossed in estate matters. "The Company has sent word," he announced, wiping his mouth with a linen napkin. "There's to be an inspection of the estate in a fortnight. We must ensure that our production numbers remain high."

Emily stirred her tea, saying nothing.

Whispers of the Tea Leaves

Henry barely noticed her silence. "I'll be in the fields today, overseeing the workers. I expect you to remain occupied with the estate accounts."

Emily nodded absently, but her thoughts were already elsewhere.

She needed to return to the tea fields.

A Step Beyond the Estate

As soon as Henry left for the fields, Emily slipped away from the bungalow, making her way toward the small thatched huts where the workers lived. She had never ventured this far before—this was not a place for a British lady. But she could no longer ignore the pull that drew her closer.

The village was alive with quiet activity—women grinding rice, children playing barefoot in the dust, the scent of wood smoke rising from clay hearths. Emily hesitated at the entrance, aware of the curious glances cast her way.

Then, she saw him.

The tea worker, the man whose presence had unsettled her, intrigued her. He stood at the edge of the village, speaking with an elder. His expression was calm but firm, his voice steady.

Whispers of the Tea Leaves

Emily took a breath and stepped forward.

As if sensing her presence, he turned. Their eyes met, and something passed between them—an acknowledgment, an understanding.

She opened her mouth to speak, but before she could, a voice interrupted.

"Memsaab," Mr. Hastings called from behind her, his tone polite but laced with authority. "I believe the master is expecting you back at the bungalow."

Emily's heart lurched. She turned to see the overseer standing at a distance, watching her closely. His meaning was clear—this was not her place.

She stole one last glance at the tea worker, then, without another word, turned and walked away.

But in her heart, she knew this was not the last time they would meet.

A Forbidden Brew

That evening, when the estate had fallen into stillness, Emily did something reckless.

She retrieved the tea leaves from her desk and brewed them in secret, just as she had seen the tea worker do.

Whispers of the Tea Leaves

She used no milk, no sugar, only the boiled water and the raw leaves.

As the steam curled upward, she brought the cup to her lips and took a slow sip.

It was unlike anything she had ever tasted—bold, rich, untamed, the essence of Assam itself.

Emily placed the cup down, her fingers trembling slightly.

This was not just a drink.

This was a choice.

And there would be no turning back.

Chapter Five:
Boundaries and Breaches

Jitu Mishra

The tea fields stretched before Emily like a rolling sea of green, the morning mist still clinging to the delicate leaves. The estate was waking, its rhythm familiar—workers moving through the fields in synchronized motion, the overseers riding along the dirt paths, their presence a quiet reminder of order.

Emily stood on the verandah of the bungalow, her fingers tightening around the porcelain tea cup in her hands. But this time, she was not drinking the tea served by the estate—this was the tea she had brewed in secret the night before.

The taste lingered on her tongue, a stark contrast to the processed, milky brew she had been given at every meal since her arrival. There was something real about it, something untouched. And for the first time, Emily felt as though she had crossed an invisible threshold—one that separated her from the world she had always known.

An Invitation of Defiance

As the day unfolded, Emily found herself walking the same narrow path toward the tea fields, drawn once more to the land and the people who toiled upon it. The village still whispered in her thoughts, the scent of woodsmoke and earth more vivid than the polished wood and perfume of the estate.

She had barely reached the first row of tea bushes when a shadow moved in the periphery of her vision.

Jitu Mishra

He was there.

The tea worker, standing beneath the shade of a neem tree, his posture calm but alert, as if he had been expecting her.

Emily hesitated. The rules were unspoken but firm—she was not meant to be here, not meant to speak to him. But something about his presence made the rules feel thinner, weaker.

He stepped forward, his dark eyes unwavering.

"You drank it."

It was not a question.

Emily's breath caught. She had not told anyone about the tea.

She nodded. "Yes."

Something flickered across his face—satisfaction, perhaps? Recognition?

Then, to her surprise, he lifted his hand and opened his palm. More tea leaves, fresh, unprocessed.

A silent offering.

Emily hesitated only a moment before stepping forward, her fingers brushing against his as she took them. The touch was fleeting, barely there, but it sent a ripple through her. This was not just an exchange of leaves—it was an unspoken invitation.

Whispers of the Tea Leaves

An Overseer's Watchful Eye

A cough shattered the moment.

Emily spun, her heart hammering against her ribs. Mr. Hastings stood a few feet away, his expression unreadable, though his eyes told her everything.

She had been seen.

The overseer's voice was polite, but firm. "Mrs. Davenport, the master has asked for you at the bungalow."

Emily turned back, but the tea worker was already gone, his presence dissolved into the landscape as though he had never been there.

She clenched the leaves in her fist, then nodded. "Of course, Mr. Hastings."

As she walked back toward the estate, she did not look back.

But inside, she knew this was far from over.

Henry's Warning

Henry was waiting for her in the study, standing by the window, his hands clasped behind his back.

"Emily," he said without turning, "why were you in the fields?"

Whispers of the Tea Leaves

She chose her words carefully. "I wanted to see the workers."

He turned then, his expression unreadable. "They are laborers, not your concern."

Emily felt something tighten in her chest. "If I am to be your wife, if I am to live here, shouldn't I know the land? The people?"

Henry's jaw tightened. "The people are workers, Emily. They are not equals, not friends. Do not mistake their silence for innocence."

She held his gaze, refusing to shrink beneath his words.

After a long moment, Henry sighed and stepped closer. His voice softened, but it carried an edge. "For your own sake, stay where you belong."

Emily lowered her eyes, not in submission, but to hide the anger simmering beneath her skin.

She would do no such thing.

A Choice is Made

That night, when the estate had once again settled into stillness, Emily unwrapped the tea leaves from her palm.

She traced the edges of each leaf, knowing that she was standing at a crossroads.

Whispers of the Tea Leaves

There were rules. Expectations. A life that had been carved for her before she had even stepped foot in Assam.

And then, there was the tea. The land. The man whose presence unsettled her, intrigued her.

She set the kettle over the fire and watched as the water began to boil.

She had already made her choice.

Chapter Six:
The Storm Within

Jitu Mishra

The wind carried the scent of damp earth and crushed tea leaves as dark clouds gathered over the horizon. The monsoon was approaching, its presence felt in the heaviness of the air, the restless movement of the trees.

Emily stood at the edge of the verandah, watching the sky shift above the tea fields. The air was charged, thick with the promise of rain.

Inside, Henry's voice echoed from the study. "The Company is increasing demands. We need higher yields before the rains make it impossible to harvest."

Another storm—one of trade, power, and control—loomed inside the walls of the estate.

Emily clutched her shawl tighter around her shoulders. She had made a choice, a silent one, marked by the tea leaves she had brewed in secret. But choices did not remain unnoticed forever.

She could feel the shift, a quiet unraveling of the world she had once belonged to.

An Unexpected Meeting

Later that afternoon, as she walked toward the storage sheds, she noticed movement beyond the plantation—a familiar figure near the jungle's edge.

The tea worker.

He was standing near a wooden shelter where workers took refuge from the midday sun, speaking to a group of laborers. Their expressions were serious, their voices hushed.

Emily hesitated, but something in his stance pulled her forward.

As if sensing her, he turned.

Their eyes met, and for a moment, the rest of the world faded—the estate, the rules, the watchful eyes.

Then he did something unexpected.

He raised his hand, gesturing for her to follow.

The Heart of the Plantation

Emily had never been this far into the estate, beyond the carefully maintained paths, past the rows of orderly tea bushes.

Here, the plantation felt different—wilder, untouched.

The workers moved freely, without the rigid discipline enforced under British eyes. Their laughter, their voices, the scent of freshly plucked leaves—it was the heartbeat of the land.

Whispers of the Tea Leaves

The tea worker led her to a small clearing beneath a large banyan tree, where a group of workers sat in a loose circle, passing around clay cups of tea.

Emily hesitated, but the tea worker gestured toward a seat.

"Stay," he said simply.

She lowered herself onto the woven mat, her fingers curling around the warm earthen cup handed to her.

The tea was nothing like what she had tasted before. It was strong, rich, and smoky, its heat grounding her in this unfamiliar moment.

She glanced at the tea worker. He was watching her, not with suspicion, but as if waiting to see if she truly belonged here.

And for the first time, she realized—perhaps she did.

Hastings' Shadow

The moment shattered when a shadow moved at the edge of the clearing.

Emily turned sharply—Mr. Hastings.

He stood at a distance, arms crossed, his expression carefully unreadable.

Whispers of the Tea Leaves

The workers fell silent, their conversation dissolving into the rustling of the trees.

Emily slowly placed the cup down. She knew what this meant.

Hastings had been watching.

And soon, Henry would know.

A Brewing Storm

That night, the rains finally came.

Thunder rumbled over the valley as sheets of water lashed against the windows of the estate.

Emily sat in her room, staring at the silk handkerchief on her desk, still holding the tea leaves he had given her.

A storm had broken outside.

And she knew—another was about to break within these walls.

Chapter Seven:
The Gathering Storm

Jitu Mishra

The storm had passed, leaving the air thick with the scent of wet earth and tea leaves. The tea bushes, weighed down by the rain, glistened under the morning sun, but the estate was anything but peaceful.

Emily stood near the verandah, her fingers brushing against the silk handkerchief in her pocket. The tea leaves hidden within felt heavier than before—a reminder of the path she had chosen.

She could no longer ignore the tension growing around her. Something had shifted.

Henry's Silence

At breakfast, Henry barely spoke. He sat at the head of the table, his hands wrapped around a porcelain tea cup, his gaze distant.

Emily studied him carefully. He had not mentioned Mr. Hastings, had not asked why she had gone to the workers' village. But she could feel it—a storm brewing beneath his silence.

She sipped her tea, the taste now foreign, processed, stripped of its essence. Not like the tea she had brewed in secret.

Finally, Henry spoke, his voice measured.

Jitu Mishra

"The Company's inspectors will be here next week. I expect everything to be in order."

Emily nodded, waiting for something more, but he only turned his attention back to his tea.

She knew then—he was waiting. Watching.

A Warning in the Fields

Later that afternoon, Emily wandered the estate, her steps taking her toward the tea fields without thought. The sky was still heavy with clouds, the aftermath of the storm lingering in the air.

Then she saw him.

The tea worker, standing beneath a tree, his gaze steady as he watched her approach.

She hesitated, glancing around—they were no longer unseen.

Mr. Hastings had noticed. Henry had noticed.

And yet, she did not turn away.

When she reached him, he spoke first. "You should not be here."

Jitu Mishra

Emily's breath hitched at the quiet warning in his voice. "Neither should you," she said softly.

A shadow of something—concern, perhaps?—flickered across his face.

"The overseer is watching," he said, his voice barely above a whisper. "And so is your husband."

Emily clenched her fingers around the handkerchief in her pocket. She had known this moment would come. She had just not expected it so soon.

"I don't care," she whispered back.

The tea worker held her gaze for a long moment, his dark eyes unreadable. Then, with deliberate slowness, he reached into his satchel and pulled out a small pouch of tea leaves.

"Then take this," he murmured.

Emily hesitated before taking the pouch, their fingers brushing briefly.

A silent exchange, a promise without words.

She tucked the tea into the folds of her saree and turned, walking away without another word.

She did not need to look back to know he was still watching her.

Whispers of the Tea Leaves

Jitu Mishra

The Unspoken Accusation

That evening, as Emily returned to the bungalow, she found Henry waiting for her in the sitting room.

He stood by the window, the last remnants of daylight casting a shadow over his face. His tea sat untouched on the side table.

She barely had time to remove her shawl before he spoke.

"You've been spending a great deal of time in the fields."

Emily froze.

She turned slowly, meeting his gaze. His voice was even, but his words carried an edge.

"I walk the estate," she said, carefully. "As you suggested I should."

Henry's lips pressed into a thin line. He did not look convinced.

"There are places you do not belong, Emily." His voice was softer now, but no less dangerous. "I hope you understand that."

Emily's fingers curled against the folds of her saree, feeling the hidden pouch of tea leaves beneath the fabric.

She forced a smile. "Of course."

Henry held her gaze for a moment longer, then turned back toward the window.

Emily left the room without another word, but she knew—Henry had already made up his mind.

And the storm was far from over.

Chapter Eight:
A Dangerous Invitation

Jitu Mishra

The morning air was thick with the scent of damp tea leaves, the ground still slick from the previous night's rain. The estate was quiet, but beneath the surface, something had shifted.

Emily had felt it at breakfast—Henry's gaze sharper than usual, Mr. Hastings more watchful than before. There was an unspoken warning in the way the servants averted their eyes when she walked past.

And yet, when she found the small folded note beneath her bedroom window, her pulse quickened.

She unfolded the parchment, her fingers trembling slightly.

"Tonight. By the banyan tree."

There was no signature. There didn't need to be.

The Invitation She Could Not Ignore

That night, Emily slipped out of the bungalow, careful not to wake the servants. The monsoon clouds had cleared, leaving behind a sky streaked with silver and shadow.

She moved quickly through the estate, past the neat rows of tea bushes, until she reached the outskirts of the plantation, where the land grew wilder, untamed.

Jitu Mishra

And there he was.

The tea worker stood beneath the massive banyan tree, his posture relaxed but his gaze alert. The moonlight caught the contours of his face—strong, sharp, unreadable.

For a long moment, neither of them spoke. Then, in a voice low and steady, he said:

"You should not have come."

Emily lifted her chin. "You sent for me."

His lips twitched—not quite a smile, not quite approval. "And yet, you came."

She stepped forward, closing the space between them. "Why?" she asked. "Why now?"

The tea worker studied her for a moment, then reached into a small cloth pouch tied at his waist. He pulled out something and held it between his fingers.

A single wild tea leaf, different from the cultivated ones on the plantation.

"This," he said, "is the tea your empire is trying to claim."

Emily frowned, reaching out to touch the leaf. "This isn't like the ones I've seen before."

Jitu Mishra

She swallowed hard. "Why show me this?"

His eyes held hers. "Because you are not like them."

She exhaled, stepping closer. "And what does that make me?"

For the first time, a ghost of a smile touched his lips.

"Someone who has a choice."

A Warning from the Shadows

Before she could respond, a rustling sound broke the stillness of the jungle.

The tea worker tensed, his eyes flickering toward the shadows.

Emily turned sharply, her heart pounding.

A figure stood just beyond the trees.

Mr. Hastings.

He did not step forward, nor did he call out.

But his meaning was clear.

He had seen her.

And tomorrow, so would Henry.

Chapter Nine:
The Name in the Shadows

Whispers of the Tea Leaves

The air was thick with the scent of rain-drenched earth as Emily hurried back to the bungalow, her heart pounding against her ribs. She could still feel the weight of his words, the wild tea leaf pressed between her fingers.

But none of it mattered now.

She had been seen.

Mr. Hastings had not called out, had not followed her, but his presence had been enough. A warning. A silent promise that whatever had transpired in the jungle would not remain a secret for long.

Emily knew Henry would hear of it soon. And when he did, everything would change.

A Reckoning Over Breakfast

The next morning, the dining room was silent except for the clink of silverware. Henry sat across from her, his tea untouched, his expression unreadable.

Emily forced herself to drink, the taste of processed, over-boiled tea now unbearable after what she had experienced the night before.

Finally, Henry spoke. "Hastings tells me you were wandering near the jungle last night."

Emily's fingers tightened around the porcelain cup. "I couldn't sleep. I went for a walk."

Whispers of the Tea Leaves

Henry's gaze sharpened. "A walk. In the middle of the night?"

She met his stare evenly. "I needed air."

He set his cup down, the sound louder than necessary. "I know what you're doing, Emily."

A chill ran down her spine. "And what is that?"

Henry leaned forward, his voice dropping to a dangerous whisper. "You think I don't see it? The way you linger in the fields? The way you look at them?"

Emily's pulse quickened, but she refused to lower her gaze.

"They are people, Henry," she said, her voice steady. "Not shadows in the fields."

Henry scoffed. "They are workers. And they belong where they are."

Emily exhaled sharply, pushing back from the table. "Perhaps that's what you believe. But I am not you."

She left the room before he could say another word, before he could see how much she was shaking.

A Name Finally Given

Emily found him in the fields, just as the sun began its slow descent behind the hills.

The tea worker stood alone, inspecting the leaves, his hands moving with practiced ease. He did not look up when she approached.

She stopped a few feet away, watching him. "Mr. Hastings saw us."

He plucked a leaf from the branch, rolling it between his fingers. "I know."

Emily hesitated. "I don't regret it."

Now he looked at her. "You should."

She took a step closer. "If I regretted it, I wouldn't be here."

A flicker of something crossed his face—caution, curiosity, something deeper.

For the first time, she asked, "What is your name?"

He exhaled slowly, as if weighing the decision.

Then, at last, he answered.

"Rajveer."

Emily repeated it softly, letting it settle. Rajveer.

It felt like something forbidden, something neither of them should have shared.

And yet, in that moment, it belonged only to them.

A Gift and a Warning

Rajveer reached into his satchel and pulled out a small wooden box.

He held it out to her. "Take it."

Emily hesitated before taking the box, her fingers brushing against his. She opened it carefully—inside were dried wild tea leaves, the kind he had shown her beneath the banyan tree.

"This is what tea should taste like," he said. "Not what they serve in the estate."

Emily closed the box and looked at him. "And what happens if they find this?"

Rajveer's jaw tightened. "Then they will know you've chosen a side."

A gust of wind rustled the tea bushes around them, carrying the scent of something untouched, something unspoiled.

Emily exhaled.

She had already chosen.

Whispers of the Tea Leaves

The Storm Gathers

That night, Emily sat by her window, the wooden box of tea in her lap.

In the distance, she could see the lights of the overseer's quarters, where Henry and Hastings were likely discussing her.

She knew Henry would not let this go.

And she knew Rajveer had put himself at risk just by speaking his name aloud.

But as she opened the box and ran her fingers over the dried leaves, she felt something else—a quiet certainty.

A storm was coming.

And she was no longer afraid.

Chapter Ten:
The Breaking Point

Jitu Mishra

The rain had returned by morning, drumming softly against the wide windows of the bungalow. The air smelled of wet soil and crushed tea leaves, heavy with something unspoken.

Emily sat at her dressing table, brushing her hair absentmindedly, her thoughts circling the wooden box tucked away in her drawer.

She had made a choice.

And soon, she would have to answer for it.

A Confrontation in the Sitting Room

Henry was waiting for her in the sitting room, his back turned as he stared out at the plantation beyond the rain-streaked glass. A cup of tea sat untouched beside him, the steam curling in the air.

Emily stepped inside, the weight of the silence pressing against her.

Finally, he spoke.

"You met him again, didn't you?"

She didn't flinch. "Who?"

Henry turned, his eyes dark with something she had never seen before. Anger. Betrayal. Fear.

"Don't play games with me, Emily," he said, his voice sharp. "You've been seen. Hastings told me everything."

Her fingers clenched around the folds of her saree. "Everything?"

Henry exhaled harshly. "I should have stopped this sooner."

She took a step forward. "Stopped what, Henry?"

His jaw tightened. "This...this fantasy that you could walk among them. That you could—" He stopped, as if saying it aloud would make it real. "This has to end."

Emily lifted her chin. "You don't own me."

A muscle in Henry's cheek twitched. "No. But I own this estate. And I own them."

She took another step closer, her voice steady. "And that's the problem, isn't it?"

For the first time, Henry hesitated.

She saw it—the flicker of doubt. The smallest crack in his certainty.

Then, just as quickly, it was gone.

"This is your last warning," he said, his voice lowering. "Stay away from him."

Whispers of the Tea Leaves

Emily held his gaze for a long moment. Then, she turned and walked out of the room, leaving the tea untouched on the table.

She had already tasted something better.

A Secret Meeting in the Storm

The rain had slowed to a drizzle by nightfall, the sky a deep shade of indigo.

Emily pulled her shawl tightly around her shoulders as she slipped out of the bungalow, her heart hammering.

She had to see him.

She made her way to the far edge of the plantation, where the fields met the jungle. The scent of damp tea leaves clung to the air, mixing with the distant hum of insects.

And then—he was there.

Rajveer.

He stepped out from the shadows of the trees, his expression unreadable.

"You shouldn't have come," he said.

Emily ignored the warning in his voice. "Henry knows."

Rajveer exhaled, running a hand through his rain-damp hair. "Then it's not safe for you anymore."

A pause. Then:

"And yet, here you are."

Emily took a step closer. "I trust you."

Rajveer's gaze flickered to hers, something shifting between them—something fragile, something real.

"Trust can be dangerous," he murmured.

She held his gaze. "So can silence."

For a long moment, neither of them moved. The air between them felt alive, charged with something neither of them dared to name.

Then, before either could speak—

A branch snapped in the darkness.

Rajveer's body tensed instantly. Emily turned sharply, her pulse spiking.

From the shadows, a figure emerged.

Mr. Hastings.
His expression was one of quiet triumph.

Jitu Mishra

"Didn't I warn you, Memsahib?" he said, his voice smooth. "You're playing a very dangerous game."

Emily's breath caught in her throat.

Rajveer moved protectively beside her, his shoulders squared.

Hastings' gaze flickered to him. "And you..." He shook his head slowly. "You just made the biggest mistake of your life."

The rain began to fall again.

And this time, there was no escape.

Chapter Eleven:
The Colonial Rush Begins

The monsoon had passed, but the air still carried the weight of something unfinished, unresolved. The tea bushes glistened in the morning light, lush, untouched, thriving. But Emily knew it would not last.

Change was coming.

A New Arrival at the Estate

Emily had not seen Rajveer since that night in the rain. Since they had been caught.

Mr. Hastings had not spoken of it—yet. But Henry had grown colder, his patience thinning. There were no more warnings now. Only silence.

And then, the letter arrived.

A summons from the East India Company.

Henry read it over breakfast, his expression unreadable.

"They're sending an official," he said, setting the letter down. "To assess expansion."

Emily froze. "Expansion?"

Henry looked at her, his lips curling slightly. "It's happening, Emily. Assam will be the new tea empire. We're just getting started."

Her fingers tightened around her cup.

Jitu Mishra

The forests. The land. The people.

All of it—sacrificed for tea.

The Clearing of the Forests

That afternoon, the first trees fell.

Emily stood on the verandah, watching as workers hacked away at the thick jungle, stripping the land bare.

Smoke curled into the air as they burned what could not be uprooted.

She felt sick.

She thought of the wild tea trees Rajveer had shown her, thriving long before the British arrived. The ones that needed no interference.

And yet, the Company would not settle for what already existed. They needed control. Order. Ownership.

And the land—like its people—had no say in its fate.

The Arrival of the Indentured Workers

A week later, they came.

Emily stood at a distance as a caravan of men, women, and children arrived at the estate—indentured workers from Central India.

Jitu Mishra

Their clothes were worn, their bodies thin, their expressions hollow.

Henry stood at the forefront, arms crossed, overseeing the new arrivals.

"They'll work harder than the locals," he murmured. "They have no choice."

Emily's stomach twisted. No choice.

She watched as the overseers marked each worker, registering them in a ledger.

Debt would keep them here. If not theirs, then their children's. And their children's children.

A cycle. A trap.

A Silent Encounter

That night, as Emily walked along the plantation's edge, she saw a figure standing near the workers' quarters.

Her breath caught.

Rajveer.

He stood in the shadows, watching the new arrivals, his expression unreadable.

She hesitated, then took a step toward him.

Jitu Mishra

"You knew this was coming," she whispered.

Rajveer didn't look at her. "I've seen it before."

Emily swallowed. "And?"

Now, he turned. His eyes, dark and filled with something heavy, met hers.

"And I know what happens next."

She exhaled sharply. "Then tell me."

For a long moment, he was silent. Then—

"They will be worked to the bone. Some will die. Some will run." His voice was low, firm. "But none will leave."

Emily's pulse quickened. "Then we have to do something."

Rajveer's expression didn't change. "And what is it you think we can do, Memsahib?"

Emily flinched at the title.

"Stop calling me that."

His gaze held hers. "What should I call you, then?"

Emily swallowed. "Emily."

For the first time, Rajveer's lips twitched—not quite a smile, but something close.

Then, just as quickly, he stepped back into the shadows.

She knew he would not wait for an answer.

And she knew, deep down—he was right.

The system had been built too strong, too deep.

And yet, she could not turn away.

Chapter Twelve:
A Love That Grows in the Shadows

Jitu Mishra

The nights in Assam were different now. Quieter, heavier, charged.

The monsoon had passed, but something else lingered in the air. Something unspoken.

Emily could feel it whenever she walked through the tea fields, whenever her fingers brushed against the leaves, whenever her eyes searched for him in the distance.

And when she found him, it was never by chance.

A Meeting Beneath the Moon

The first time she saw him after that night, it was past midnight.

She had left the bungalow, following the winding path through the plantation, drawn by something she didn't quite understand.

And then—he was there.

Standing beneath a tall tea tree, his silhouette half-lit by the moon.

She hesitated. "I wasn't looking for you."

Rajveer tilted his head slightly. "But you found me anyway."

Emily exhaled, stepping closer. "Why do you always disappear?"

He studied her for a long moment. Then, with quiet finality, he said, "Because you don't belong here."

She swallowed hard. "And yet, here I am."

Rajveer's expression didn't change, but something in his posture softened. "You shouldn't be."

But neither of them moved.

And neither of them left.

The Taste of Something Real

A few nights later, she found herself in the workers' quarters.

Not inside—but standing near the edge, hidden in the shadows, watching.

She had never been this close before. Never seen the small fires flickering as the workers sat together after long days, never heard the soft murmur of a world that existed outside the estate's control.

And then, a voice behind her.

"You shouldn't be here, Memsahib."

She turned sharply.

Rajveer.

Whispers of the Tea Leaves

She exhaled. "Don't call me that."

His lips twitched slightly. "What should I call you, then?"

She hesitated. "Emily."

For a moment, they just stood there, watching each other.

Then, Rajveer stepped past her and reached into a small satchel at his side. He pulled out a handful of dried tea leaves.

Not the kind from the estate. The wild ones.

He held them out. "Taste."

Emily frowned. "They're not brewed."

Rajveer smiled faintly. "Real tea doesn't need to be drowned in boiling water to show its strength."

She hesitated, then took a leaf between her fingers. She placed it on her tongue, expecting bitterness.

Instead—something rich, something raw.

She looked at him in surprise.

Rajveer's gaze was steady. "Now you understand."

And for the first time, she truly did.

Whispers in the Fields

Days passed.

Then weeks.

And soon, Emily and Rajveer's stolen moments were no longer accidents.

They spoke in hushed tones beneath the banyan tree, their words guarded but their silences louder.

She learned things she was never supposed to know.

The truth about the indentured workers, how their contracts were a lie.

The reality of the land stolen from Assamese tribes, now turned into plantations.

The knowledge that the British didn't discover tea in Assam—they took it.

And through it all, Rajveer watched her carefully.

Because he knew—the more she learned, the less she would be able to look away.

The Suspicion Begins

But Henry was watching too.

Jitu Mishra

At first, his silence had been his weapon.

But now, his patience was thinning.

One evening at dinner, his voice cut through the quiet.

"You spend a lot of time walking the fields, Emily."

She didn't look up from her plate. "It's peaceful."

Henry set his fork down. "Peaceful. That's an interesting word for it."

Emily finally met his gaze. Cold. Unforgiving. Suspicious.

She held her breath.

And for the first time, she wondered—did he already know?

The Promise of Another Meeting

That night, Emily found a single dried tea leaf left near her window.

A sign.

She traced the veins of the leaf with her fingers, exhaling slowly.

She would go.

She would find him again.

And she would not turn back.

Chapter Thirteen:
A Line Crossed

Whispers of the Tea Leaves

The tea leaf was still in her hand when the first rays of dawn broke through the window.

Emily had held it for hours, tracing its veins, feeling the weight of its meaning.

She knew what it was—a message. A summons.

And she knew that by answering it, she would be crossing a line she could never return from.

A Journey Through the Mist

She left before the estate stirred.

Slipping past the overseers' quarters, she followed the hidden path Rajveer had shown her weeks ago.

The mist curled low over the tea fields, wrapping around her ankles like a whispered warning.

For the first time, she was not walking as the wife of the estate's owner.

For the first time, she was walking as something else entirely.

A Secret in the Jungle

Rajveer was waiting.

He stood beneath the same banyan tree, arms crossed, watching her approach.

Emily exhaled, feeling the shift between them.

"You came," he murmured.

She stepped closer. "You left me no choice."

A flicker of something—not quite a smile, but close.

He reached into his satchel, pulling out a small brass tin.

"Do you know what this is?" he asked.

Emily shook her head.

Rajveer popped it open. Inside—tiny black pellets. Twisted and rolled, unlike any tea she had seen before.

"This is tea as it should be," he said. "Not the kind they crush and burn."

She picked one up, rolling it between her fingers. "Where did you get this?"

His jaw tightened. "From those who refused to sell their land. Before they were forced out."

The words landed heavily between them.

Emily looked up at him, truly seeing him for the first time.

"You don't just work on this plantation," she whispered.

Rajveer held her gaze. "No, Memsahib. I fight for it."

A Dangerous Truth

The realization settled like a stone in her chest.

She had suspected. But now, she knew.

Jitu Mishra

Rajveer was more than just a worker.

He was part of the resistance.

Emily inhaled sharply. "If Henry finds out—"

"He won't." His voice was steady. Too steady.

Emily took a step forward. "You think I would tell him?"

Rajveer studied her for a long moment.

Then, quietly—"No."

The air between them shifted again.

Not just two people from different worlds. Two people standing on the edge of something impossible.

And yet—here they were.

The Sound of a Gunshot

Before either could speak—

A crack split the air.

A gunshot.

Emily froze.

Rajveer's eyes darkened. "Go."

She didn't move. "What's happening?"

Rajveer grabbed her wrist—not gently, not carefully. Urgently.

Jitu Mishra

"Go back. Now."

Emily turned, but it was too late.

Through the mist, a figure emerged.

Henry.

Standing on the ridge, a rifle in his hands.

Chapter Fourteen:
Shadows of Betrayal

Whispers of the Tea Leaves

The air between them shattered.

Emily barely had time to react before Rajveer grabbed her wrist, pulling her behind him.

"Henry," she gasped.

Her husband stood at the edge of the ridge, his rifle steady, his face unreadable.

For a moment, no one moved.

Then—Henry spoke.

"Step away from him, Emily."

His voice was eerily calm. Too calm.

Emily's pulse pounded. She had been caught.

But it was not just her own fate that was at stake.

She glanced at Rajveer. His jaw was clenched, his body tense.

She had seen him like this before. Like a man ready to fight.

"Henry, put the gun down." Her voice wavered, but she forced herself to hold her ground.

Henry tilted his head, studying her like she was a stranger.

"Do you know what people will say about you?" His voice was quiet, laced with something dangerous.

Emily's fingers curled into her palms. "I don't care."

Henry exhaled, shaking his head. "You will."

Then—the rifle shifted.

Not toward her.

Toward Rajveer.

The Choice That Changes Everything

Rajveer didn't flinch.

Emily did.

She stepped in front of him.

A single movement. A single choice.

Henry froze. "Move."

Emily lifted her chin. "No."

For the first time, something flickered in Henry's expression. Doubt.

Emily saw it, and she knew—she had crossed a line she could never step back from.

And so had Henry.

Jitu Mishra

His voice was colder now. "You are my wife."

Emily inhaled sharply. "I was."

A Sudden Escape

The words had barely left her lips when Rajveer moved.

Fast.

In a single motion, he grabbed her hand and pulled her toward the jungle.

Henry cursed, raising his rifle—but Rajveer was faster.

They disappeared into the trees.

The sounds of the plantation faded behind them.

Emily didn't look back.

She had made her choice.

The Sanctuary of the Forest

They ran until the gunshots faded.

Until the only sounds were the rustling of leaves and the pounding of her own heartbeat.

Rajveer finally stopped beneath a thick canopy of trees.

Emily doubled over, gasping for breath.

When she looked up, he was watching her.

"You didn't have to do that," he said.

Emily wiped the sweat from her brow. "Yes. I did."

A long silence.

Then, Rajveer exhaled, running a hand through his hair. "You realize what you've done?"

Emily met his gaze. "I saved you."

A beat.

Then—Rajveer laughed.

It wasn't amusement. It was disbelief.

Emily straightened. "What?"

He shook his head. "No, Memsahib." He let out a breath. "You just destroyed your own life."

Emily's heart hammered.

Maybe he was right.

But for the first time in her life—she felt free.

Chapter Fifteen:
A World Unknown

Jitu Mishra

The jungle was alive in a way Emily had never known.

It pulsed with movement, sounds, whispers. Every rustling leaf, every distant call of an unseen bird, felt like a reminder—she was no longer in Henry's world.

She was in Rajveer's.

A Path Without Return

They walked for hours.

Emily's saree was damp with sweat, her shawl tangled with leaves, but she didn't complain.

She didn't ask where they were going.

She already knew—wherever it was, it wasn't back.

At last, Rajveer stopped by a stream, kneeling to drink.

Emily hesitated, then followed, cupping the water in her hands.

It was cool, crisp, untouched. Unlike anything on the estate.

Unlike her old life.

When she looked up, Rajveer was watching her.

"You don't belong here," he said softly.

Emily let the water drip from her fingers. "Neither do you."

Rajveer exhaled. "No. But I have nowhere else."

A silence stretched between them.

Then—"And you?"

Emily lifted her chin. "I chose this."

For the first time, Rajveer didn't argue.

The Village of Secrets

By nightfall, they reached a small village, hidden deep in the forest.

Huts made of bamboo and thatched roofs lined the clearing. A fire crackled at the center, surrounded by people—men, women, children.

They weren't British. They weren't plantation workers.

They were the ones who had refused.

As they stepped forward, murmurs rose. Curious. Guarded.

An older woman, her silver hair pulled back in a braid, stepped forward. Her gaze lingered on Emily.

Rajveer bowed his head slightly. "She is with me."

A beat of silence.

Then—the woman nodded.

Whispers of the Tea Leaves

Without another word, she turned and walked away. The others followed.

Emily's heart pounded. That was it?

Rajveer glanced at her. "They'll let you stay. For now."

She swallowed. For now.

A Fire Between Them

That night, Rajveer sat by the fire, his arms resting on his knees.

Emily sat across from him, watching the flames dance.

"You never told me how you ended up on the plantation," she said quietly.

Rajveer didn't answer right away.

Then—"It was never supposed to be permanent."

Emily frowned. "Then why stay?"

His jaw tightened. "Because sometimes, running isn't enough."

Emily thought of Henry. Of the life she had left behind.

She understood.

"Tell me about them," she said instead. "The people here."

Whispers of the Tea Leaves

Rajveer exhaled. "They are the ones the British couldn't break."

Emily felt a shiver crawl up her spine.

Then, softly—"And you?"

For the first time, Rajveer met her gaze fully.

"I'm still deciding."

A Promise in the Dark

Later, when the fire had burned low, Emily stood, brushing the dust from her saree.

She hesitated, then looked at him.

"Will you ever leave?"

Rajveer's fingers curled around a stone. He tossed it into the dying flames.

"If I do, it won't be alone."

Emily's breath caught.

For a moment, they were just two people in the night, caught between past and future.

Then, quietly, she turned toward her hut.

But before stepping inside, she glanced back.

Rajveer was still watching the fire.

And Emily knew—this was only the beginning.

Jitu Mishra

Chapter Sixteen:
The Test of Belonging

The village awoke before dawn.

Emily did not.

She stirred only when the sounds of women grinding grains, the distant laughter of children, and the rhythmic beat of wooden pestles against stone mortars drifted through the thin walls of her bamboo hut.

For a moment, she forgot where she was.

Then—it all came rushing back.

She sat up, heart pounding, staring at the woven mat she had slept on. Not a grand bed, not silk sheets, not a mansion filled with servants.

Just a mat. Just the jungle. Just this new life.

And the question that had followed her all night: Would they let her stay?

A Village That Watches

When she stepped outside, they were already watching her.

Not unkindly. But not welcoming, either.

Women carried water pots from the stream, balancing them on their heads with practiced ease. Children wove through the huts, their bare feet kicking up dust. Men prepared hunting tools, talking in hushed voices.

And through it all, they glanced at her.

Curious. Skeptical. Waiting.

Whispers of the Tea Leaves

Then—Rajveer appeared.

He carried a bundle of firewood, his dhoti slightly damp from the morning dew. When he saw her, he did not smile.

"You should eat," he said simply.

Emily hesitated. "And then?"

Rajveer's dark eyes held something unreadable. "Then, you work."

Emily understood.

This was not a place for spectators.

If she wanted to stay—she had to belong.

The Test Begins

They gave her the simplest task.

Grinding rice into flour.

An elderly woman handed her a wooden pestle, motioning toward a large stone mortar already filled with rice.

Emily had seen the servants do this before. It looked easy.

It was not.

The weight of the pestle surprised her. It was heavy, awkward. The first time she brought it down, the grains barely moved.

Whispers of the Tea Leaves

Someone snickered.

She ignored it, adjusting her grip.

She tried again.

And again.

And again.

By the tenth attempt, her arms ached. Sweat trickled down her back.

She looked up.

The women around her were still watching.

Not laughing anymore. Just waiting.

Waiting to see if she would keep going.

She inhaled, tightened her grip, and kept going.

The First Signs of Acceptance

By midday, her hands hurt.

Blisters had begun to form, her fingers raw from gripping the pestle too tightly.

And yet—she had finished.

The elderly woman who had given her the task walked over. She inspected the flour.

Then, without a word, she scooped some up and placed it in Emily's hands.

A test.

Emily brought it to her lips and tasted it.

She didn't know what she had expected—something bitter, something unfamiliar.

But instead—it was soft. Warm. Nutty.

Like something she had always known, but never truly understood.

When she looked up, the woman gave a slight nod.

A small one. But it was there.

And for the first time since she had arrived, Emily felt like she had taken the first step toward belonging.

Rajveer's Warning

That evening, as the sun dipped behind the trees, Emily found Rajveer by the river.

She knelt beside him, watching as he cleaned his hands in the cool water.

"They let me work today," she said.

Rajveer's lips twitched slightly. Not quite a smile.

"Then you are already doing better than I expected."

Emily frowned. "You didn't think I would last?"

Rajveer exhaled. "I thought you would leave the moment your hands hurt."

Jitu Mishra

Emily rolled her sore fingers.

"They still hurt," she admitted.

Rajveer's gaze flickered to her hands. For a moment, something passed between them.

Then—his expression hardened.

"This is only the beginning, Memsahib."

Emily's chest tightened. She knew.

But she also knew something else.

"I'm not leaving."

Rajveer studied her for a long moment.

Then, quietly—"We'll see."

Chapter Seventeen: Deeper into the Fire

The village still did not trust her.

Emily could feel it in the glances that lingered too long, in the hushed voices that faded when she walked past.

She had worked alongside them. She had bled for this place, sweated for it.

And yet—she was still the outsider.

She had thought the hardest part was escaping Henry.

She had been wrong.

New Challenges, New Barriers

The next morning, she woke to a different kind of work.

Not grinding rice, not small chores.

Something harder.

The women led her deep into the jungle, to a clearing where long stalks of bamboo were stacked in piles.

One of the younger girls handed her a thick knife.

Emily blinked. "What is this for?"

The older woman beside her—the same one who had tested her flour—tilted her head toward the bamboo.

Emily looked down at the knife again. Realized.

They wanted her to cut. Strip. Shape.

Jitu Mishra

She swallowed hard. This was no longer a test of patience. This was survival.

If she was going to live here, she had to build.

A Moment Alone with Rajveer

She worked until her arms ached, sweat trickling down her spine.

But she did not stop.

It was near midday when Rajveer appeared.

He stood at the edge of the clearing, watching her.

Emily wiped her forehead, gripping the knife tightly. "Come to tell me I'm doing it wrong?"

Rajveer stepped forward, crouching beside her. "You're not holding it right."

Before she could argue, his hands closed over hers.

For a moment, the world stilled.

His skin was rough, calloused from years of labor. Her hands, once soft, were slowly becoming like his.

He guided her grip, tilting the knife at a better angle. "Like this. Let the blade do the work."

Emily swallowed. She was suddenly very aware of how close they were.

Jitu Mishra

She turned slightly. So did he.

For one heartbeat—there was only the sound of the jungle, the whisper of the wind.

Then—he pulled away.

Emily exhaled, not realizing she had been holding her breath.

"Thank you," she murmured.

Rajveer stood, his face unreadable. "You're not useless, Memsahib."

It was the closest thing to a compliment she had received.

And it was enough.

The Village Begins to Shift

That evening, when she returned from the jungle, something was different.

She walked past a group of women and they did not stop talking.

She caught bits of conversation—about a hunt, about the season's crops.

Not about her.

For the first time since she had arrived—they had not seen her as something separate.

Jitu Mishra

She did not smile. But inside, something softened.

Maybe, just maybe, she was starting to belong.

Henry's Shadow Looms

Far away, beyond the jungle, Henry was waiting.

And he was done being patient.

He stood on the veranda of his grand estate, a glass of whiskey in hand. His grip was too tight.

"She's still out there," he muttered.

The overseer beside him shifted uncomfortably. "The forest is vast, sir. The locals will not talk."

Henry's eyes darkened.

They thought he would just accept this? That she could just leave?

No.

He owned her.

And if she thought she could just disappear into the jungle—she was mistaken.

Henry set down his glass. "Send word to the guards. I want her found."

His voice was calm. Dangerous.

"Burn the whole damn jungle if you have to."

Chapter Eighteen:
Shadows in the Jungle

The jungle whispered of danger.

Emily felt it before she saw it—a shift in the air, the way the birds fell silent, the rustle of something unseen in the undergrowth.

She stood near the river, washing the dirt from her hands, but her mind was elsewhere. Henry had not sent anyone after her yet.

That was what worried her most.

She knew him. Silence was never a sign of surrender.

Rajveer's Warnings

"You've been uneasy all day."

Emily turned to see Rajveer standing nearby, arms crossed.

His gaze was sharp, scanning the jungle like he, too, could sense something was off.

"I know Henry," Emily murmured. "He won't let me go."

Rajveer exhaled. "The jungle is vast. He won't find you."

Emily shook her head. "He doesn't need to find me. He just needs to destroy everything in his way."

Rajveer was silent.

Then, quietly—"You think he'll burn it?"

Jitu Mishra

Emily swallowed. Yes.

And that terrified her.

A Visitor in the Night

That evening, just as the last light faded, a shadow slipped into the village.

A man, breathless, his clothes torn from running.

The village men surrounded him instantly, weapons raised.

Rajveer stepped forward. "Who are you?"

The man barely got the words out—"The British... they're coming."

The silence that followed was deafening.

The Village Prepares

Panic could have spread.

Instead, it was met with action.

The men gathered weapons—bows, spears, whatever they had. They had faced invaders before.

The women packed food, hid supplies in the jungle, whispered instructions to their children.

Emily stood in the middle of it all, frozen.

This was her fault.

Jitu Mishra

If she had never come here, the village would not be in danger.

Rajveer's Choice

"You need to leave."

Emily turned sharply. Rajveer stood behind her, face hard.

"No," she said immediately.

"This is not your fight, Memsahib."

Emily's hands clenched into fists. "It is if it's because of me."

Rajveer's expression darkened. "You don't understand. If Henry takes you back, you won't get another chance to escape."

Emily stepped closer. "And what happens to you?"

Rajveer didn't answer.

That was when she knew—he had never planned on leaving.

He would fight.

Even if it meant dying.

Emily's heart pounded. "I'm not running."

Rajveer exhaled sharply, frustrated. But in his eyes, there was something else.

Jitu Mishra

Something that scared her more than Henry ever could.

He cared.

He cared enough to send her away.

She was not going anywhere.

The Night Before the Storm

The village was quiet that night.

Too quiet.

Emily lay awake, staring at the ceiling of her hut, listening to the sounds of the jungle.

She knew Rajveer was awake too.

Somewhere outside, preparing.

Waiting.

So was she.

Because when Henry came, she would not be the woman who ran anymore.

Chapter Nineteen:
The Battle for Freedom

The First Signs of the Attack

The jungle was silent.

Too silent.

Emily stood just outside her hut, staring into the darkened trees, her breath slow and steady.

She felt it—something was coming.

A sharp whistle cut through the air. Rajveer's scout emerged from the trees, panting. His face was slick with sweat.

"They're here."

A flicker of firelight glowed through the thick jungle canopy. Torches. Marching. A storm about to break.

Rajveer turned to the villagers. "Get into position."

Men grabbed their bows, spears, and crude but deadly weapons. Women ushered children into hidden shelters, pressing warnings into their ears.

Emily did not run.

She was done running.

The British Forces Arrive

Henry stepped out of the jungle first, his coat unbuttoned, his face tight with anger. Behind him, British soldiers and mercenaries fanned out, torches in hand.

Jitu Mishra

He surveyed the village, unimpressed. Then, his eyes found Emily.

"Come now, my dear. Enough of this nonsense."

Emily's spine stiffened. The sound of his voice—the arrogance, the ownership in it—sent a pulse of anger through her.

But she wasn't alone anymore.

Rajveer stepped forward, placing himself between Emily and Henry.

"You have no right to her," Rajveer said, his voice calm but unyielding.

Henry laughed. "No right? She's my wife."

Emily took a step forward. "I am not your wife."

Something in Henry's eyes flickered. A warning. A shift from amusement to something colder.

"You can't win this," he said to Rajveer. "Step aside. This is between me and my wife."

Rajveer's fists clenched.

"She is not yours to own."

For the first time, Henry hesitated.

And then—the battle began.

The Battle Breaks Out

A gunshot split the air.

One of Henry's men fired into the trees, but the villagers were already moving.

Arrows flew. Spears hurled. The jungle came alive with shouts, the clash of weapons, the crackle of flames.

The British soldiers set fire to the village, the orange glow flickering against the bamboo huts.

But the villagers did not run.

They fought.

Emily grabbed a bucket, dousing flames, helping the wounded. Smoke stung her eyes, but she kept moving.

And then—Henry grabbed her.

The Final Showdown: Rajveer vs. Henry

He yanked her back against him, his fingers digging into her arm.

"This ends now," he hissed.

Emily twisted, slamming her elbow into his ribs. Henry staggered, stunned that she fought back.

Rajveer saw.

And he came for Henry.

Whispers of the Tea Leaves

They crashed into each other—Henry using brute strength, Rajveer using skill.

Henry swung wildly, his face contorted with rage.

Rajveer dodged, countered, struck. His fists landed where it hurt.

Henry stumbled.

He wasn't used to fighting a man who fought to protect, rather than to control.

Henry reached for a knife.

Rajveer saw the glint of metal and moved faster.

He spun, knocking the weapon from Henry's hand, sending it clattering into the dirt.

Then, with one final strike—Rajveer brought him down.

Henry hit the ground, gasping for breath, his lip split, his eyes wide.

He had lost.

Henry's Fall

The battlefield fell silent.

Henry's men watched as their leader lay in the dirt.

One by one, they backed away.

They had been promised wealth, control, an easy victory.

Whispers of the Tea Leaves

They had not expected this.

Without Henry's power behind them, they had no reason to fight.

They fled.

Rajveer stood over Henry. "Leave. And never come back."

Henry struggled to his feet, humiliated, furious. But he knew when he had lost.

With one last glare at Emily, he turned and disappeared into the jungle.

The Aftermath

The fires were doused. The village still stood.

Rajveer looked around at his people—his home.

They had won.

Emily stood nearby, her breath still heavy, her hands shaking.

Rajveer stepped toward her.

"You fought."

Emily met his gaze. "So did you."

A small, tired smile flickered across Rajveer's lips.

The village was safe.

Henry was gone.

And now—they had a future to decide.

Chapter Twenty:
The Night After the Fire

Whispers of the Tea Leaves

The Smoke Settles

The village stood, but it bore scars.

The fires had been extinguished. The wounded were tended to. The British had retreated, leaving only ashes and silence in their wake.

But Emily didn't feel relief.

She stood near the edge of the village, staring at the jungle, where the embers of the battle still glowed in the distance. Henry was gone. Defeated. But her body still trembled—not with fear, but with something heavier, something deeper.

Rajveer was beside her, silent, watchful.

"You should rest," he finally said.

Emily turned to him, studying his face. There was blood on his temple, a cut on his arm, soot smudged across his jaw.

He had fought for her.

For all of them.

And something inside her broke and mended all at once.

A Wound That Needed Tending

Rajveer exhaled, running a hand through his hair. The battle was over, but his body still carried the tension of war.

Whispers of the Tea Leaves

Emily stepped closer. "You're hurt."

"It's nothing," he muttered.

She ignored him, reaching up to touch the wound on his temple.

Rajveer flinched—but did not move away.

Emily's fingers were gentle, tracing over the cut, the warmth of his skin beneath her touch. "You say that, but you're bleeding."

His breath caught for a second.

"You care too much, Memsahib."

Emily smiled faintly. "And you pretend to care too little."

An Unspoken Confession

Rajveer stepped back, just slightly, his eyes dark and searching.

"I never asked you why you ran," he murmured.

Emily stiffened, her heart hammering. He deserved to know.

"I ran because... I was trapped." Her voice was quiet. "With Henry, I was not a wife. I was a possession. A trophy."

Rajveer's jaw clenched. "And now?"

Emily took a slow breath. "Now, I am free."

Rajveer's gaze locked onto hers.

"Then why are you still trembling?"

Emily swallowed. Because she had never felt this way before. Because he was standing too close, and she did not want him to move away.

"Because," she whispered, "I do not know what happens next."

Rajveer studied her for a long moment.

Then, slowly, he reached out.

Not to take. Not to claim.

But to simply touch.

His fingertips brushed against hers, tentative.

And Emily—for the first time in her life—leaned in.

The First Kiss

The night air was thick with the scent of rain and earth, the remnants of fire lingering in the distance.

Rajveer's hand moved to her cheek, his touch featherlight.

Emily did not pull away.

She tilted her face toward him.

Jitu Mishra

The space between them vanished.

And then—his lips met hers.

It was not desperate. Not hurried.

It was slow, deliberate, filled with everything they had not said.

Emily's hands found his chest, his heartbeat strong beneath her palms.

Rajveer deepened the kiss, pulling her closer, their bodies finally breaking the distance they had fought so hard to keep.

The jungle sighed around them. The world shrank to this moment.

Emily had never known a kiss could feel like a promise.

A choice.

A beginning.

The Morning That Follows

When Emily woke, the sun was golden against the misty jungle.

Rajveer lay beside her, his arm draped over her waist, his breath steady against her skin.

She turned slightly, watching him.

His features, normally so guarded, were peaceful in sleep.

Emily smiled, tracing her fingers lightly over his wrist.

She had thought she would never belong anywhere.

But now... she wasn't so sure.

For the first time in her life, she did not feel lost.

She felt found.

Chapter Twenty-One:
A Life Among the Tea Leaves

Morning in the Village

The first rays of the sun painted the jungle in gold, casting a warm glow over the endless green of the tea groves. Emily woke to the scent of damp earth, the sound of birds calling from the treetops, and the steady rhythm of Rajveer's breathing beside her.

For the first time in her life, she felt no weight on her chest. No expectations. No restraints.

She turned slightly, watching Rajveer as he lay beside her, still lost in sleep. His face, usually so guarded, was at peace.

Carefully, she traced a finger over the rough calluses of his hand resting on the mat. This man had fought for his people, for the land, for her.

A soft smile tugged at her lips. She belonged here. With him.

Living with the Land

The days took on a rhythm—a life so different from the structured, suffocating existence Emily had once known.

In the mornings, she and Rajveer would walk through the tea groves, where dew clung to the leaves like tiny jewels.

Rajveer taught her how to recognize the finest buds, how to pluck them gently, how to roll the leaves between her fingers to release their aroma.

**Whispers of the Tea Leaves

"Assam's tea is strong, like its people," he murmured one afternoon, handing her a fresh leaf. "It thrives in the heat, in the storms, in the wild."

Emily studied the leaf in her palm. "Then perhaps I was meant to be here."

Rajveer looked at her for a long moment before finally saying, "Perhaps you were."

A Home Among Strangers

Emily had expected to feel like an outsider among the villagers. But the people of the tea groves welcomed her with quiet acceptance.

The women taught her how to weave baskets and dry the tea leaves with care.
The children laughed as they ran through the fields, delighted when she joined their games.
The elders nodded in approval when they saw how she worked alongside them, no longer a foreign Memsahib, but a part of their world.

One evening, as she sat by the fire, an old woman handed her a steaming cup.

"This is how tea was meant to be," the woman said, her voice rich with wisdom. "Before the sahibs came."

Emily took a sip. It was unlike anything she had ever tasted—earthy, rich, alive.

A lump formed in her throat. This was Assam's tea. Its true tea. And it was disappearing.

Whispers of the Tea Leaves

She looked at Rajveer, who sat beside her, his gaze knowing. They both understood—if they did nothing, it would soon be lost.

The Strength of Two Hearts

One evening, after a long day in the groves, Rajveer and Emily walked by the river. The sky was painted in shades of crimson and gold, the water reflecting the colors like molten fire.

Rajveer reached down, plucking a wild jasmine flower from the riverbank. He turned it in his fingers before tucking it behind Emily's ear.

She smiled. "Is this an Assamese custom?"

"No." His voice was quiet. "Just something I wanted to do."

Emily reached for his hand. "What will we do, Rajveer? About the tea, about what's happening to Assam?"

He exhaled, watching the river's steady flow. "We fight. Not with weapons, but with what we know. With what we love."

Emily nodded. "Then I fight with you."

He turned to her, his dark eyes filled with something deep, something unwavering. "Always?"

She stepped closer, her hands resting against his chest, feeling the steady beat of his heart.

Whispers of the Tea Leaves

"Always."

The jungle whispered around them, the river sang, and in that moment, there was no empire, no war—only the promise of a love as strong as the land they stood upon.

Chapter Twenty-Two:
The Colors of Bihu

The Call of the Drums

The air vibrated with the rhythm of dhols, their deep beats rolling through the village like distant thunder. Emily had never heard such music before—wild, untamed, alive.

She stood near the open ground where the celebrations were about to begin. The entire village had gathered, dressed in bright red, gold, and white. Women in mekhela chadors moved gracefully, their silver jewelry catching the firelight. Men, wrapped in white dhotis and red gamusas, held drums and flutes, waiting for the dance to begin.

Rajveer stepped beside her, dressed in traditional Assamese attire. The red and white gamusa draped over his shoulder seemed like a banner of pride. He leaned in and murmured, "Bihu is not just a festival—it is the soul of Assam."

Emily swallowed, feeling an unfamiliar flutter in her chest. For the first time, she was not merely an observer of Assamese life—she was part of it.

The Dance Begins

The first sharp beat of the dhol sent a wave of energy through the crowd.

The men moved first, their bodies twisting and leaping with an effortless grace. Then the women joined, swaying to the music, their hands moving in fluid gestures. The ground beneath them pulsed with each footstep, the rhythm pulling Emily in like the current of a river.

Whispers of the Tea Leaves

Rajveer nudged her playfully. "You're staring."

Emily turned to him, laughing. "It's mesmerizing."

One of the village women, an elderly lady wrapped in golden silk, approached Emily and held out her hands. "Come, dance."

Emily hesitated. "I—I don't know how."

But the woman only smiled. "Bihu is about joy, not perfection."

Before Emily could protest, she was gently pulled into the circle of dancers. The music swelled, and the movement became instinct.

At first, she stumbled, but laughter erupted around her, encouraging, welcoming. Rajveer stepped in, his movements fluid and confident. "Just follow me," he whispered.

She did.

She followed the rhythm, the heartbeat of Assam.

And as the dance carried her forward, she realized she had never felt this free.

The Firelight and the Promise

The celebration lasted long into the night. As the dancing slowed, the villagers gathered around the fire, singing Bihu geets—songs of spring, love, and longing.

Whispers of the Tea Leaves

Emily sat beside Rajveer, breathless but exhilarated. The fire flickered in his dark eyes, casting shadows that made his features seem even sharper, more alive.

He turned to her, a teasing smile playing at his lips. "So? Are you a Bihu dancer now?"

Emily laughed. "Hardly. But I think I understand why it matters so much."

Rajveer's expression softened. "Bihu is more than a festival. It reminds us of who we are. No matter how much the world changes, we still dance, we still sing. That is how we survive."

Emily glanced at the villagers, their voices rising in unison, a melody of resilience.

She looked back at Rajveer. "Then let's make sure Assam never loses its song."

A slow smile spread across his face. "We will."

And in that moment, Emily knew that this was more than a festival.

It was a promise.

Chapter Twenty-Three:
Songs of the Land

The Melodies of Assam

The morning air was filled with the distant sound of a flute, soft and haunting, drifting from the village square.

Emily sat outside the bamboo hut, watching as the golden sun pierced through the mist. She had danced, she had laughed, she had felt a part of something larger than herself. But now, there was something new—a melody that stirred something deeper.

Rajveer emerged from the hut, tying his gamusa around his neck. He followed her gaze toward the music. "That's Keshav Dada," he said. "He sings about the land, about what it was before the plantations came."

Emily stood. "Take me to him."

The Keeper of Songs

In the heart of the village, an elderly man sat cross-legged, his pepa resting in his lap. His silver hair glistened in the morning light, his fingers tracing the wooden flute as if it were a sacred relic.

Rajveer led Emily to him. "Keshav Dada," he said respectfully, "she wants to understand our songs."

The old man studied Emily. His eyes, lined with the wisdom of time, held a quiet curiosity.

He gestured for them to sit. "You cannot understand a song until you listen with your heart." He lifted the flute to his lips, and the first note rang through the village.

Whispers of the Tea Leaves

The Song of the Tea Groves

The melody spoke of the rolling hills before the plantations, when the forests were free and the tea grew wild. It told of the rivers that carried spices, the birds that sang at dawn, the people who lived in harmony with the land.

Emily felt something tighten in her chest.

"This is not just music," she whispered. "It's history."

Keshav Dada nodded. "Before the Company came, tea was a gift of the land, not a thing to be owned. The British planted rows and rows, but they do not hear the songs in the leaves."

Rajveer spoke, his voice quiet but firm. "We must not let them take the song away."

Emily looked at him. "Then we won't."

A Song of Her Own

That evening, as the villagers gathered for another round of music, Emily sat beside Rajveer, listening.

But this time, she was not just a listener.

As the elders began a familiar tune, Rajveer nudged her gently. "Sing."

Emily hesitated. She had always been an outsider, a stranger to these melodies. But now, she had danced their dances, heard their stories, felt their struggles.

Whispers of the Tea Leaves

She took a deep breath. And she sang.

Her voice was soft at first, uncertain. But as she sang, she found something unexpected—herself.

Rajveer watched her, his eyes shining with something she had never seen before. Not admiration. Not curiosity. But something deeper. Something unspoken.

She finished the song, and the villagers clapped. Keshav Dada smiled. "Now," he said, "you have heard with your heart."

The Promise of Music

As the fire burned low, Rajveer and Emily sat together in silence.

Finally, Rajveer spoke. "Emily, will you stay?"

She turned to him. Not with surprise, not with fear—but with certainty.

"I already have."

And somewhere, in the rustling leaves of the tea groves, the land sang its own quiet song.

Chapter Twenty-Four:
The Art of Survival

The Loom and the Threads of Time

Emily ran her fingers over the delicate patterns woven into the fabric. The mekhela chador in her hands was more than just cloth—it was a story, spun from the hands of Assamese women for generations.

Rajveer's aunt, an elderly woman with silver hair tied neatly in a bun, smiled as she gestured for Emily to sit beside her. "We do not just weave fabric," she explained in Assamese, "we weave our history."

Emily watched as the old woman moved the shuttle through the loom, her hands swift and precise. The pattern of elephants and rivers, of stars and tea leaves, emerged with each pass of the thread.

Rajveer leaned over, translating as Emily listened carefully. "This is how we tell our stories when words are not enough."

Emily picked up a thread, trying to mimic the motion. Her fingers fumbled, and the thread snapped.

The women laughed softly, and one of them patted her hand. "Like anything worth knowing, it takes time."

Emily smiled, adjusting her grip. Time was something she had here. And she was willing to learn.

The Dye That Runs Through the Land

The scent of turmeric, indigo, and flowers filled the air as Emily followed the women to the riverbank.

Whispers of the Tea Leaves

Large clay pots bubbled with natural dyes, the colors rich and vibrant—deep reds from the bark of trees, golden yellows from turmeric, deep blues from indigo leaves.

Emily dipped a cloth into the red dye, watching as it darkened instantly, staining her fingers in the process.

One of the younger women laughed. "Now you are marked by Assam," she teased.

Rajveer, who stood nearby, grinned. "No turning back now."

Emily smirked. "I wasn't planning to."

The women around her nodded approvingly, handing her another piece of cloth to dye.

With each movement, Emily felt the connection grow deeper—between herself, the land, and the people who had welcomed her.

The Healing Wisdom of the Forest

Later that day, an elderly village healer led Emily through the thick, green forest. She carried a woven basket, picking leaves, roots, and flowers as she walked.

Rajveer followed closely, translating as the healer spoke. "Nature gives us everything we need. For fevers, for wounds, for pain."

Emily bent down to examine a small yellow flower. The healer nodded. "That one is for childbirth pain. And this," she pointed to a vine creeping up a tree, "is for the belly, when food is bad."

Whispers of the Tea Leaves

Emily inhaled the earthy scent of the herbs, realizing how much knowledge was hidden in the land, waiting to be remembered.

The healer placed a small pouch of dried leaves into Emily's hand. "Boil these in water. It will help you sleep."

Emily smiled, pressing the pouch to her heart. She would not just learn these things—she would preserve them.

A Promise in the Moonlight

That evening, Emily and Rajveer sat on the edge of the tea grove, looking out at the moonlit fields.

Emily held out her hands, now stained with dye and dirt from the day's work. "I don't feel like a Memsahib anymore."

Rajveer took her hands in his, turning them over gently. "That's because you're not."

Emily swallowed the lump in her throat. She had come here as an outsider, but now... this was home.

She looked at Rajveer. "These traditions, this knowledge—we have to protect them."

He nodded. "Then we will."

And under the silver glow of the moon, they made a silent promise—to each other, and to the land that had given them everything.

Chapter Twenty-Five:
The Sacred Ritual of Tea

A Hidden Tradition

Emily followed Rajveer deep into the forest, where the dense canopy of trees filtered the morning sun into golden shafts. The air smelled of damp earth, crushed leaves, and something else—something fragrant, something ancient.

Rajveer finally stopped at a clearing where a small group of villagers sat in a circle around a clay teapot resting on stones, steam curling from its spout.

An elder, his face lined with wisdom, turned to them. "You have come to witness our tea," he said in Assamese, his voice steady as the river.

Emily stepped forward, mesmerized. This was not the British tea she had known—rows of trimmed bushes, factory-dried leaves shipped to England. This was something else. Something sacred.

The Tea of the Ancestors

The elder gestured for Emily to sit. A young woman handed her a small earthen cup, still warm from the fire.

Rajveer translated as the elder spoke. "Before the British came, tea was not just a drink—it was life. The Ahoms, the Singphos, the Khamtis... we drank it for strength, for healing, for the spirit."

Emily lifted the cup to her lips. The tea was unlike anything she had tasted before—earthy, smoky, with the wild scent of the forest still clinging to it.

She looked at Rajveer, eyes wide. "This is Assam's true tea."

Whispers of the Tea Leaves

He nodded. "Not the plantations, not the factories. This is how we drank before the world tried to take it from us."

The Tea Ceremony

The elder continued, his hands moving with practiced grace. He lifted a handful of freshly plucked leaves, rolling them gently between his fingers before dropping them into the hot water.

"The British boil their tea, crush it into dust," he said. "But true tea must be alive."

Emily watched as the leaves unfurled, releasing their essence into the water. It was a ritual, a communion with the land itself.

One by one, the villagers took a sip, their silence speaking more than words.

Emily held her cup close. "This is not just tea," she whispered. "It's a legacy."

Rajveer met her gaze. "And we must protect it."

A New Vow

As they left the grove, Emily felt something shift within her. She had learned to weave, to dye, to heal—but this, this was different.

This was the heart of Assam.

She turned to Rajveer. "The British will never respect this. They will destroy it."

Whispers of the Tea Leaves

Rajveer's jaw tightened. "Not if we don't let them."

Emily took his hand. "Then we fight for it."

The leaves rustled in the wind, as if the land itself had heard their promise.

And in that moment, Emily knew—this was not just about love.

It was about survival.

Chapter Twenty-Six:
The Rising Storm

The British Push Deeper

Emily stood at the edge of the plantation, her eyes tracing the red markings on the trees. The surveyors had been here, driving their wooden stakes into the ground—signs that the British were claiming more land.

Rajveer arrived, his expression tense. "They are pushing past the river now. The governor wants more land cleared for new plantations."

Emily exhaled sharply. "That means more villages will be uprooted."

Behind them, a group of villagers watched anxiously. An elderly woman whispered, "Where will we go? Our fathers lived here, and their fathers before them."

Rajveer's jaw clenched. "They will not stop unless we stop them."

Emily turned back to the forest. This wasn't just about tea anymore. It was about survival.

Whispers in the Bazaar

The market in town was buzzing with unease.

Merchants sat behind stalls, selling spices, rice, and silk, but their eyes darted around cautiously. People were talking in hushed voices.

Emily and Rajveer moved through the crowd, listening.

A trader whispered, "They're bringing more workers from Bengal, Bihar—indentured laborers. The British are tricking them with false promises."

Whispers of the Tea Leaves

Another added, "They don't know what's waiting for them in these plantations."

Emily's stomach tightened. "They're not just replacing the locals. They are turning this land into a prison."

Before Rajveer could respond, a British officer approached, his boots kicking up dust. His pale blue eyes lingered on Emily.

"Memsahib," he said, tipping his hat. "You've been keeping interesting company."

Emily met his gaze without flinching. "I prefer those who don't steal from the land."

The officer smirked. "Careful, Mrs. Davenport. You wouldn't want to forget where you belong."

But Emily already knew where she belonged.

The Plantation Turns Into a Prison

The tea gardens no longer smelled of promise—they smelled of sweat, pain, and fear.

Emily walked through the fields, watching rows of workers bent under the scorching sun. Their backs glistened with sweat, their hands raw from plucking leaves.

A child coughed violently, struggling to keep up. He couldn't have been older than eight.

The overseer raised his bamboo stick. "Faster, you rats!"

Emily's voice rang out. "Enough!"

Whispers of the Tea Leaves

The overseer turned, sneering. "These workers must earn their keep, Memsahib."

Rajveer stepped forward, his voice like steel. "They are not slaves."

The overseer chuckled. "Aren't they?" He gestured toward a row of huts. "They are in debt. They work. If they cannot work, they die. It's simple."

Emily felt sick. This wasn't a plantation. This was a machine built to break people.

She met Rajveer's gaze. "We have to stop this."

A Secret Gathering

That night, in the safety of a hidden grove, villagers gathered. Farmers, traders, elders—faces lined with exhaustion, but also with quiet defiance.

Emily stepped forward. "The British will not stop until there is nothing left for us."

An elderly man shook his head. "But how can we resist? They have guns. We have nothing."

Rajveer's voice was steady. "We have knowledge. We know this land, this tea. The British need us more than we need them."

An old woman, her hands rough from years of work, lifted her chin. "They took our forests. They will not take our tea."

Emily looked at Rajveer. There was no fear in his eyes. Only resolve.

She reached for his hand. "Then we fight."

The fire crackled, sending embers into the night. The British thought they had already won.

They were wrong.

Chapter Twenty-Seven:
The First Blow

The Plan Takes Shape

The flickering light of the oil lamp cast shadows across the wooden walls of the hut as Emily, Rajveer, and a group of villagers gathered in secrecy. The air smelled of damp earth and chai, but beneath it all was a current of tension and urgency.

Rajveer spread a crude map on the floor, his finger tracing a path through the tea estate. "This is where we strike."

Emily studied the markings. "We have to be careful. If the British discover this..." She let the thought trail off.

An elder nodded. "We strike where it will hurt them most—the tea shipments."

A younger worker clenched his fists. "They treat us like animals. It's time they feel our pain."

Rajveer looked at the faces around him. Fear, yes. But also fire. Determination. The storm had begun.

The Sabotage Begins

The night was thick with fog as Emily and Rajveer moved through the plantation, their steps silent. Behind them, a small group of workers followed, their hearts pounding in unison.

Near the storage shed, Rajveer gave a silent signal. Two men crept forward, cutting the ropes that secured the heavy tea chests.

Emily knelt near the equipment. With steady hands, she loosened the wooden supports of the drying racks.

Jitu Mishra

The sound of cracking wood echoed in the silence.

A voice hissed, "Guards!"

Rajveer grabbed Emily's hand and pulled her behind a stack of crates.

Footsteps approached. A lantern swung dangerously close.

Rajveer held his breath. Emily's fingers curled around his wrist. If they were caught now...

But the guard muttered something and moved on.

Rajveer exhaled. "We're not done yet."

A Message to the British

Dawn broke over the plantation, revealing the destruction.

Crates of tea lay shattered, their contents spilled into the dirt like wasted gold.

The drying racks had collapsed, ruining an entire batch of leaves.

The overseers shouted, scrambling to contain the damage. A British officer stormed toward the main bungalow, his face red with fury.

Inside, the governor sat in his leather chair, turning a tea cup absently in his fingers. "Who did this?"

An overseer stammered, "The workers. They are rebelling."

Jitu Mishra

The governor's eyes darkened. "Then we make an example of them."

Retaliation

By mid-afternoon, British soldiers had arrived.

They dragged workers into the courtyard, their faces bloodied from beatings.

Emily and Rajveer watched from a distance, rage and helplessness burning in their chests.

A British officer addressed the workers. "For every act of sabotage, you will suffer tenfold."

He turned to the guards. "Teach them a lesson."

Emily felt sick. The workers had struck the first blow, but the British would not back down easily.

Rajveer's voice was a whisper. "This is just the beginning."

Emily nodded. "Then we fight harder."

As the sun set over the burning tea fields, the battle for Assam had truly begun.

Chapter Twenty-Eight:
The Uprising Spreads

A Night of Fire and Fury

The full moon cast a pale glow over the tea plantation as shadows moved silently between the bushes. Rajveer led a group of workers, their eyes burning with quiet rage.

Emily crouched beside him, whispering, "We strike only at their supply chains. No lives should be lost."

Rajveer nodded. "We fight for our people, not for blood."

With practiced precision, the workers set fire to the storage barns, where sacks of dried tea leaves were stacked high, ready to be shipped to Calcutta. The flames spread quickly, the dry wood catching like paper.

A worker smashed open crates, spilling tea onto the ground. Another severed ropes that secured shipments to waiting carts.

Then, the warning bell rang.

"Run!" Rajveer ordered.

The group scattered into the forest as British guards stormed the plantation, rifles in hand.

A gunshot rang out. A worker cried out and fell.

Emily's heart pounded as Rajveer grabbed her hand, pulling her deeper into the trees. The fight had begun.

The British Retaliate

By morning, smoke still curled from the ruins of the storage barns.

Jitu Mishra

British officers stormed through the village, dragging men from their homes, accusing them of treason.

The overseer barked, "You will pay for what you did!" He struck a villager across the face.

Emily rushed forward. "He was with me last night. He had nothing to do with this."

The British officer turned to her, eyes cold. "Do not interfere, Memsahib."

Emily refused to back down. "You call this justice? Beating innocent men?"

The officer smirked. "If they are innocent, then they will have no problem working without pay. Let's see how long they last."

Rajveer clenched his fists. "We must get them out."

Emily whispered, "We will."

The British thought they could break the workers. But they had underestimated Assam's spirit.

A Plan to Strike Back

Deep in the forest, Rajveer and Emily gathered with a group of rebel workers.

A young boy, no older than fourteen, looked up with wide eyes. "They took my father."

An old man, his voice filled with quiet fury, said, "They have turned us into slaves."

Jitu Mishra

Emily's voice was firm. "We will not let them win."

Rajveer spread a map over a tree stump. "The next shipment leaves in three days. We take it before it reaches the river."

A woman asked, "And then?"

Emily met Rajveer's gaze. "Then we send a message they will never forget."

The fire in their eyes was no longer fear. It was war.

The Ambush at the River

The sound of rushing water filled the air as Rajveer and his men lay in wait near the riverbanks.

Emily peered through the foliage. A caravan of bullock carts rolled toward the docks, crates of tea stacked high.

Rajveer raised his hand. A silent command.

The workers moved swiftly, cutting ropes, overturning carts. Tea spilled into the river like waves of defiance.

A British guard shouted, "Attack!"

Gunshots rang out.

Rajveer knocked a rifle from a soldier's hands. Emily swung a wooden staff, striking an officer before he could grab a worker.

The British were outnumbered. One by one, they retreated.

Rajveer turned to Emily. "We did it."

But Emily's face was pale. "They will come back."

And they would. With a vengeance.

Chapter Twenty-Nine:
The Last Stand

Jitu Mishra

The British Prepare for a Final Strike

The tea plantation was eerily silent. It was the kind of silence that came before a storm.

Inside the governor's bungalow, a group of British officers gathered around a map, their faces tense.

"The rebels have struck again," an officer said, slamming his fist on the table.

The governor exhaled, swirling his tea in a delicate porcelain cup. "Enough of these games." His voice was cold. "Burn their villages. Arrest their leaders. Make an example of them."

The officers saluted. By nightfall, the British attack would begin.

Emily and Rajveer's Last Stand

Deep in the Assamese forest, Emily, Rajveer, and the villagers sat around a fire, knowing this might be their last night of freedom.

An elder spoke softly. "We have survived the forests, the rivers, the storms. We will survive them."

Rajveer looked at Emily. "You don't have to stay. You could escape now."

Emily's gaze didn't waver. "And leave you? No."

She reached for his hand. In that moment, there were no British or Assamese—only two souls, bound together by love and rebellion.

Jitu Mishra

The Attack on the Village

Before dawn, gunshots shattered the silence.

Emily bolted upright as flames erupted in the distance.

Rajveer grabbed his sword. "They're here."

Villagers ran through the smoke-filled air as British soldiers stormed in, dragging men and women from their huts.

A soldier grabbed a child—Rajveer swung his weapon, knocking him down.

Emily fought beside him, using a wooden staff to block an officer's attack.

They were outnumbered, but they fought with the strength of those who had nothing left to lose.

Rajveer is Captured

A gunshot rang out.

Rajveer stumbled, blood staining his arm.

Emily screamed as soldiers surrounded him, striking him down.

A British officer sneered. "Your rebellion is over."

Emily lunged forward, but strong arms held her back.

Through the chaos, Rajveer met her gaze. "Live."

Emily shook her head. "Not without you."

Jitu Mishra

But before she could reach him, he was dragged away.

Tears blurred her vision. This was not the end. It could not be.

Escape and a New Plan

Under the cover of smoke, villagers pulled Emily into the forest.

"We have to go back for him!" she cried.

An elder grasped her shoulders. "If you are captured too, who will fight for him?"

Emily's breath hitched. Rajveer was in chains. The village was burning. But the war was not over.

She wiped her tears. "Then we free him."

The fire of rebellion burned brighter than ever.

As she turned to face the rising sun, she knew—this was only the beginning.

Chapter Thirty:
London's Love for Tea

Whispers of the Tea Leaves

A World Away from Assam

Far from the burning plantations of Assam, in the heart of London, a grand estate stood in perfect order.

Inside, chandeliers sparkled, and delicate porcelain teacups clinked as guests gathered in the parlor of Lord William Harrington—Emily's father.

The table was set with fine china, silver spoons, and an array of scones, biscuits, and clotted cream. Steam curled from freshly brewed Assam tea, its rich amber color glowing in the candlelight.

A guest smiled, lifting her cup delicately. "Truly, nothing compares to the tea from India."

Lord Harrington nodded. "The finest in the empire."

Another aristocrat, a stout man in a waistcoat, leaned forward. "And I hear production is expanding?"

A man in a military uniform spoke, "There has been some... unrest."

Lord Harrington waved a hand. "A few discontented natives. Nothing the Company cannot handle."

The room filled with polite chuckles. They drank their tea, blissfully unaware of the blood spilled for every leaf.

Emily's Absence is Noticed

Lady Eleanor, Emily's mother, sat silently, stirring her tea.

A guest leaned in. "Lord Harrington, how is dear Emily? It's been some time since we saw her."

Lady Eleanor's hand tightened on her spoon.

Lord Harrington forced a smile. "She has taken an interest in India. She writes often—about the culture, the landscapes…"

He did not mention that her letters had grown increasingly scarce.

Lady Eleanor met her husband's gaze. She knew something was wrong.

Whispers of Rebellion

Across the room, a young man in a crisp East India Company uniform lowered his voice. "Governor Mitchell has issued a crackdown in Assam. Some of the plantations have been… damaged."

A noblewoman frowned. "How dreadful. But surely the British have it under control?"

The officer hesitated. "It seems there is a woman involved. A memsahib stirring trouble."

Lady Eleanor's spoon slipped from her fingers. It clattered loudly against the porcelain.

The room fell silent.

Lord Harrington's jaw clenched. "Ridiculous. A British woman would never associate with rebels."

Jitu Mishra

But Lady Eleanor's heart pounded in her chest.

She already knew the truth.

Her daughter was in danger.

A Letter Arrives

That night, in the study of their grand home, a letter arrived—torn at the edges, the ink smudged.

Lady Eleanor opened it, her fingers trembling.

Dearest Mother,
By the time you read this, I may already be hunted. I have seen what the British are doing to Assam. I cannot close my eyes to it. I cannot return to London and pretend these fields do not run red with suffering. I do not expect you to understand, but I need you to know—I am fighting for something greater than myself.

If you ever loved me, do not try to find me. Do not try to bring me home. This is where I belong now.

Emily.

Lady Eleanor clutched the letter to her chest.

Tears welled in her eyes.

Her daughter had chosen Assam. Chosen the rebellion. Chosen love.

Lord Harrington stared at the letter, his face cold. "She has disgraced us."

But Lady Eleanor whispered, "She has found her truth."

And in that moment, she knew—Emily was never coming home.

Chapter Thirty-One:
The Letter That Shook London

The Secret Slips Out

The next morning, London awoke to a scandal.

The front page of The Times bore the headline:

"A British Woman Among the Rebels: The Untold Truth of Assam's Tea Plantations"

Beneath it, Emily's letter was published in full.

By midday, parlors, gentlemen's clubs, and drawing rooms across London buzzed with whispers and speculation.

At Lord Harrington's estate, a furious argument erupted.

"How did this get out?" Lord Harrington's voice thundered through the study.

Lady Eleanor stood by the window, the newspaper trembling in her hands.

"Perhaps she wanted the world to know the truth," she said softly.

Her husband turned on her. "This will ruin our name. Our connections."

Lady Eleanor looked him in the eye. "Our daughter is in danger, and all you care about is your reputation?"

The Public Reacts

In London's tea houses and grand estates, Emily's letter sparked debate.

Jitu Mishra

At the Reform Club, a young politician tapped the newspaper. "We claim to civilize India, yet we enslave its people."

A factory owner scoffed. "She exaggerates. The plantations are a success."

In a small bookshop, a woman whispered to her husband, "Perhaps we have been blind."

In the House of Commons, members of Parliament debated whether the East India Company had gone too far.

And in private meetings, Company officials conspired to silence the scandal.

Emily had done the unthinkable—she had made Britain question its empire.

A Father's Choice

Lord Harrington sat in his private club, a glass of brandy in his hand.

Across from him, Sir Charles, a high-ranking Company official, leaned forward.

"We need to bring Emily back. She must retract her statement."

Lord Harrington's face was unreadable. His daughter had defied him. Exposed him. Shamed him.

And yet, somewhere deep in his heart, he knew she was telling the truth.

But was he willing to admit it?

Sir Charles's voice turned cold. "If she refuses, we will make sure she disappears."

Lord Harrington's grip tightened on his glass.

For the first time, he had to choose between his empire and his daughter.

A Mother's Resolve

That night, Lady Eleanor packed a small bag.

She placed Emily's childhood locket inside.

Her maid watched, confused. "Milady, where are you going?"

Lady Eleanor straightened her spine.

"To find my daughter before the British do."

With one final glance at her home, she stepped into the night—heading for India.

Chapter Thirty-Two:
The British Crackdown in Assam

The Company's Retaliation Begins

Smoke drifted over the hills of Assam. The British had responded to the rebellion with merciless force.

Emily crouched in the shadows of the forest, watching as red-coated soldiers stormed the villages.

Huts were set ablaze, men and women dragged into chains. The overseers marched into the plantations, cracking whips against the backs of workers, forcing them to toil harder.

From a distance, Emily saw a British officer hold up a wanted poster.

It bore her face.

"Find the Memsahib. Dead or alive."

Emily's breath caught. The Company had declared war on her.

Rajveer in Chains

At the British camp, Rajveer knelt on the ground, his wrists shackled.

Governor Mitchell stood over him, his boots sinking into the dirt. "You led them. You turned my workers against me."

Rajveer lifted his chin. "We are not your workers. We are free people."

Mitchell smirked. "You were free. Now, you will serve."

Jitu Mishra

A soldier lashed Rajveer's back. He gritted his teeth, refusing to cry out.

The governor knelt beside him. "Your Memsahib fights for you. How romantic."

Rajveer's muscles tensed. He knew Emily was still out there, planning his rescue.

But how much time did she have?

Emily's Dangerous Gamble

Under the cover of night, Emily and the rebels gathered near the prison camp.

"This is impossible," one of them whispered. "The British outnumber us."

Emily's hands tightened around the map.

"Then we make them believe we're stronger than we are."

She turned to a group of villagers. "Set fires on the hills. Beat the war drums. Make them think an army is coming."

The rebels nodded.

Emily met the eyes of a young boy holding a dagger. "Stay back. This is not your fight."

The boy lifted his chin. "It is now."

Her heart ached. Too many had suffered. This had to end.

Jitu Mishra

The Escape

The first fires lit up the night sky.

From inside the British camp, officers scrambled. "They're coming!"

In the confusion, Emily slipped inside the prison barracks.

She found Rajveer, his wrists raw from the shackles.

"You're late," he whispered, smirking despite his wounds.

She smiled. "Let's go."

Together, they fought their way through the camp— Emily striking down a guard with the butt of a rifle, Rajveer knocking another unconscious with his bare fists.

As they reached the riverbank, British soldiers spotted them.

Gunfire rang out.

Emily and Rajveer dived into the river, the cold water pulling them downstream.

Bullets pierced the surface, but they did not stop swimming.

They had escaped. But the fight was far from over.

A Ship from London

On the other side of the ocean, a ship cut through the waters of the Bay of Bengal.

Jitu Mishra

Lady Eleanor stood at the bow, gripping the railing.

She was days away from Calcutta. From Assam. From Emily.

She had abandoned her title, her wealth, her reputation.

But she would find her daughter.

And she would bring her home.

Chapter Thirty-Three:
A Mother's Journey

Arrival in Calcutta

The steamship docked at the bustling port of Calcutta. Lady Eleanor stepped onto the wooden pier, the humid air pressing against her skin.

The city buzzed with energy—rickshaws weaved between British carriages, Bengali traders haggled over silk and spices, and in the distance, the grand offices of the East India Company loomed over the city like a silent predator.

She adjusted her hat and turned to the man beside her—Captain James Hawthorne, an old friend of her husband.

"You must reconsider, Eleanor," he said, his voice firm. "India is dangerous for a woman alone."

She met his gaze. "My daughter is here. That is all that matters."

Hawthorne sighed. "If she is mixed up in this rebellion, the British will not be merciful."

Lady Eleanor's jaw tightened. She had not come to plead for Emily's return—she had come to stand by her.

Whispers of the Rebel Memsahib

Lady Eleanor made her way through the city's crowded streets, seeking information.

At a small tea shop, she overheard a conversation.

A merchant poured steaming tea into delicate clay cups. "The Memsahib of the Rebels escaped," he whispered.

Jitu Mishra

Another man leaned in. "They say she freed a native prisoner. The Company is furious."

Lady Eleanor's heart pounded. Emily was alive.

But the British were hunting her.

An Unexpected Ally

That night, in the dim light of her rented lodging, a knock sounded at the door.

She opened it to find a young Assamese man, his eyes sharp with caution.

"You are Emily's mother?"

Her breath caught. "You know my daughter?"

The man nodded. "She fights for us. She is with Rajveer."

Lady Eleanor exhaled shakily. She had never heard that name before, but something in his tone told her— Rajveer was important.

"Take me to her."

The man hesitated. "It is too dangerous."

She straightened. "If she is willing to risk her life for Assam, then I am willing to risk mine for her."

The man studied her for a long moment, then nodded. "We leave at dawn."

Jitu Mishra

The Journey to Assam

The next morning, Lady Eleanor set out on horseback, leaving Calcutta behind.

Through dense jungles, across rushing rivers, past tea plantations where workers toiled under the Company's watchful eye—she traveled deeper into the Assam hills.

At night, she slept beneath a sky thick with stars, the cries of distant animals filling the silence.

For the first time, she saw the land through Emily's eyes. It was beautiful, wild, untamed—and worth fighting for.

As she neared the rebel hideout, a thought lingered in her mind.

Would Emily still want to see her?

Chapter Thirty-Four:
Reunion in the Wild

Through the Jungle

The thick Assam jungle hummed with life—crickets chirped, leaves rustled, and somewhere in the distance, a river roared.

Lady Eleanor rode through the dense foliage, gripping the reins tightly. Her body ached from days of travel, but her heart pounded with anticipation.

At last, her guide—the young Assamese man—slowed his horse. "We are close."

Eleanor peered ahead. Through the mist, she could see huts made of bamboo and dried palm leaves, hidden among the trees.

Her breath hitched. Emily was here.

A Daughter Transformed

As they entered the village, whispers followed her. A British woman, here?

Then, Emily emerged from one of the huts.

Her hair was unbound, her skin sun-kissed, her clothes no longer those of an Englishwoman. She wore a simple Assamese mekhela chador, a dagger at her waist, and in her arms—a bundle of fresh tea leaves.

For a long moment, mother and daughter simply stared at each other.

Then, Emily's voice—quiet, cautious. "Mother?"

Jitu Mishra

Lady Eleanor dismounted, her knees weak, her voice a whisper. "My Emily."

Emily looked at the villagers, at Rajveer standing nearby, before turning back to her mother.

"Why are you here?"

A Tense Conversation

Inside Emily's hut, an oil lamp flickered between them.

Lady Eleanor took in the humble surroundings. No crystal chandeliers, no velvet curtains—only simplicity, warmth, and purpose.

She spoke first. "Your letter reached London. The world knows about Assam now."

Emily's eyes darkened. "And yet, nothing has changed."

Lady Eleanor sighed. "The British will not surrender easily. But neither will you."

Emily studied her mother. She had expected anger, disappointment—but instead, she saw something else. Understanding.

"You crossed an ocean for me," Emily whispered.

Lady Eleanor smiled, brushing a strand of hair from her daughter's face. "I crossed an ocean because you showed me the truth."

Jitu Mishra

Rajveer and Lady Eleanor Meet

Later that evening, Rajveer approached cautiously.

Lady Eleanor observed him—the man who had captured her daughter's heart.

He bowed slightly. "It is an honor, Memsahib."

She studied him, then smiled. "Call me Eleanor."

Emily let out a small laugh. Rajveer looked relieved.

For the first time, Emily felt something she hadn't in months—peace.

But that peace would not last.

Outside, a scout ran into the village, breathless.

"The British are coming."

Emily rose to her feet instantly, her heart pounding.

Lady Eleanor turned to her daughter. "Then I will fight beside you."

The final battle was near.

Chapter Thirty-Five:
The Final Stand

The British Army Approaches

Dawn had not yet broken when a low, rumbling sound echoed through the valley.

From the hills above the tea estates, Emily, Rajveer, and Lady Eleanor watched as British forces marched forward —hundreds of red-coated soldiers, armed with rifles, flanked by mounted cavalry.

The governor rode at the front, his face cold as stone. "We crush the rebellion today."

Behind him, a line of captured villagers, including women and children, were bound in chains.

Emily clenched her fists. This wasn't just about tea anymore. This was about survival.

Rajveer turned to the gathered villagers, his voice steady. "This is our land. They take our crops, our freedom, our people. Today, we take it back."

Lady Eleanor, standing at his side, lifted her rifle. "We fight together."

The Battle Begins

A sharp whistle pierced the air.

From the forest, villagers emerged—armed with bows, spears, farm tools, anything they could wield.

The British fired first. Gunshots cracked, smoke filling the air.

Jitu Mishra

Emily ducked behind a tree, loading her revolver. She had never been a soldier, but she would not run.

Rajveer moved like a shadow—knocking a rifle from a soldier's hands, striking with precision.

Lady Eleanor fired, hitting a British officer who had raised his sword against a villager.

The battle raged across the hills, the scent of gunpowder mixing with the earth.

Then, the tide shifted.

A group of villagers cut through the enemy lines, freeing the captives.

The British ranks broke.

The governor, still on horseback, saw the chaos unfold. "Fall back!"

The British retreated.

The village had won.

A Costly Victory

Smoke curled in the morning air.

Bodies lay on the battlefield—some British, some villagers. Not all had survived.

Emily stood beside Rajveer, bruised, exhausted, but victorious.

Jitu Mishra

Lady Eleanor wiped dirt from her face. "You did it."

Rajveer shook his head. "We all did."

The British had been defeated, but they would return.

Emily knew that their fight wasn't over. But today, they had proved something—the people of Assam would not bow.

The Future of Assam

Days later, Emily and Rajveer stood among the tea bushes.

The land, once ruled by the British, now belonged to its people again.

"The British will come back," Rajveer said softly.

Emily nodded. "And we will be ready."

Lady Eleanor smiled at them both. "The world will hear your story."

Emily turned to Rajveer, taking his hand.

"Whatever happens next, we face it together."

And in that moment, beneath the Assam sky, surrounded by the land they had fought for, they knew—this was only the beginning.

Chapter Thirty-Six:
A New Dawn

The World Reacts

The rebellion in Assam sent shockwaves across the British Empire.

In London, newspapers printed bold headlines:

"Uprising in the Tea Plantations – A British Woman Among the Rebels!"

In Parliament, politicians argued fiercely over the East India Company's brutal methods.

Some defended the empire's rule, but others—influenced by Emily's letter and the growing unrest—began questioning the morality of British colonialism.

The Company's grip on Assam had not yet broken, but the first cracks had appeared.

The Birth of a New Tea Culture

Far from London's debates, Emily and Rajveer stood on the lush green hills of Assam.

The land had changed hands—not in law, but in spirit.

Rajveer bent down, his fingers brushing the wild tea bushes. "The British brought plantations, but tea has always been ours."

Emily nodded. "Let's grow tea the way it was meant to be —without chains, without cruelty."

Jitu Mishra

Together, they worked with the villagers to cultivate native tea—grown in freedom, not under British rule.

Slowly, the first leaves of their rebellion took root.

Lady Eleanor's Decision

One evening, as the sun dipped into the horizon, Lady Eleanor sat alone, staring at the rolling hills.

Emily approached, sitting beside her.

"Are you thinking of going back?"

Her mother sighed. "London is no longer my home. But I am not certain Assam is either."

Emily took her hand. "You changed everything when you came here. You don't have to leave."

Lady Eleanor smiled softly. "Perhaps I will stay a little longer."

For the first time, she felt at peace—not as a woman of London, but as a mother, a friend, and an ally to this land.

The Final Sip

That night, Emily and Rajveer sat outside their small hut, a steaming pot of tea between them.

The rebellion had ended, but their journey was far from over.

Jitu Mishra

Rajveer poured two cups—one for Emily, one for himself.

He lifted his in a quiet toast. "To freedom."

Emily met his gaze, a smile playing at her lips. "To the future."

The scent of fresh Assam tea drifted into the night, whispering of a new beginning.

Epilogue:
The Legacy of the Leaves

Many Years Later

The Assam sky stretched wide, golden light spilling over the rolling hills of tea plantations.

A young boy ran barefoot between the tea bushes, his laughter echoing in the morning air.

Near a wooden house on the hill, Emily and Rajveer stood side by side, watching their son play.

His dark Assamese eyes were filled with the same fire Rajveer once had. His soft golden curls were a reminder of Emily's past.

Emily smiled, taking Rajveer's hand. "The future belongs to him now."

Rajveer nodded. "And we have given him a land that is free."

A Letter from London

Inside their home, an old, yellowed letter rested on a wooden shelf.

It was from Lady Eleanor.

She had returned to London—not to reclaim her former life, but to tell the truth.

She had written books, spoken to Parliament, and exposed the cruelty of the British tea trade.

Jitu Mishra

The East India Company had begun to crumble, pressured by the voices of those who could no longer look away.

And though she lived an ocean away, she never stopped writing to her daughter.

Her final letter, before she passed away, had ended with:

"I have seen the world change, my dearest Emily. And you—more than anyone—have changed it."

The Tea That Changed the World

Years later, a small ship docked in London, its cargo carefully wrapped in handwoven Assamese cloth.

Inside, a special batch of tea—grown without masters, without overseers, without blood.

On the label, written in bold letters:

"Rajveer & Emily's Assam Tea – Cultivated in Freedom"

In a quiet teahouse in the heart of London, a woman lifted a steaming cup to her lips.

She took a sip, closed her eyes, and tasted not just the tea, but the revolution behind it.

The whispers of the past lingered in every leaf, carrying a story of love, struggle, and liberation.

Jitu Mishra

Final Words

Emily and Rajveer's story became legend— whispered in the markets of Assam, debated in the halls of London, and remembered in every sip of tea.

The land they fought for continued to thrive, free from British rule.

And though time passed, the leaves never forgot their whispers.

The whispers of freedom.

The whispers of love.

The whispers of the tea leaves.

Jitu Mishra is a historian, archaeologist, and storyteller passionate about bringing India's rich past to life. As co-founder of Sarna Educational and Cultural Services, he has authored several books exploring India's heritage. His latest novel, Whispers of the Tea Leaves, blends history, love, and rebellion in colonial Assam.

Whispers of the Tea Leaves

A story of love, rebellion, and freedom in 19th-century Assam

In the heart of British-controlled Assam, where sprawling tea plantations mask a world of cruelty and oppression, Emily Davenport, a British woman, dares to challenge the empire she was born into. Drawn by the land's untamed beauty, she finds herself entangled in the lives of the local Assamese people—especially Rajveer, a tea plantation worker turned revolutionary.

What begins as an act of quiet defiance soon turns into a full-fledged rebellion. As the British tighten their grip, Emily and Rajveer risk everything to fight for the freedom of their people and their land. Amidst burning plantations, daring escapes, and whispered secrets over cups of stolen tea, their love becomes both their greatest strength and their deepest vulnerability.

But when the British strike back with ruthless force, tearing them apart, Emily must decide—will she return to the comforts of London, or will she stand and fight for the land that has become her true home?

From the misty hills of Assam to the grand tea parlors of London, Whispers of the Tea Leaves is a gripping historical romance that unfolds against the backdrop of the colonial tea trade. It is a tale of passion, resistance, and a love that defied an empire.